Look not mournfully into the Past. It comes not back again. Wisely improve the Present. It is Thine. Go forth to meet the shadowy future, without fear, and with a manly heart.

Hyperion, A Romance *by Henry Wadsworth Longfellow*

I0639712

Sweetwater Secrets

Heather Rhodes

Published by Heather Rhodes, 2023.

This is a work of fiction. Similarities to real people, places, or events are entirely coincidental.

SWEETWATER SECRETS

First edition. September 22, 2023.

Copyright © 2023 Heather Rhodes.

ISBN: 979-8989216123

Written by Heather Rhodes.

Luke and Ethan, you are my greatest blessings, and I dedicate this book to you with all the love in my heart. May it be a small testament to the enduring bond we share and the endless possibilities that await you.

Prologue

Twenty-three years ago

She sat back against the tree, the rough bark biting into her tender skin. She looked at him, wondering what he was thinking. They sat at the edge of a clearing, the dark verdure of the timber giving way to the soft light that bathed the dew-tipped grass. A gentle breeze blew through the treetops, rustling the leaves. Clouds were rolling in, and she could see lightning flashing in the distance. It was late spring, and the wheat crop was looking good this year.

"Have you told anyone else about the baby yet?" he asked, looking off into the distance.

"No. Just you," she answered, her voice shaking. He knew her well enough to know what she was thinking. He could probably hear the fear in her voice, but she was strong enough to not let it show in her body language. He turned to look at her, enveloping her slender hand in his.

"I'm with you whatever you decide," he softly said. "Nothing has changed between us."

Tears welled up in her eyes as he drew her to him.

1

"Charlie Joe!" her mother called. "Don't you be late for lunch again, ya hear, child?"

"Yes ma'am," she answered as she turned and ran down the church steps. The blue gingham dress and the ribbon in her long, blond hair were worn to please her momma. The torn tennis shoes were her badge of rebellion. Jeremiah Stone had sat behind Charlie Joe during the long and sometimes boring Sunday service. His pappy was a good friend of her pappy's as they worked together on the river. When the last "Amen" was said and the pastor dismissed the congregation, Jeremiah quietly slipped out the side aisle behind Charlie Joe. Dressed in his Sunday best, he struggled to keep up with her as she raced down the dirt road toward home. The echo of her momma's warning sang in his ears. His momma had died of cancer the year before.

"Slow down, Charlie Joe!" he yelled. She kept going as if she didn't hear him. Nobody in school ran faster than Charlie Joe. She looked back over her shoulder as she cut into the timber at the edge of the road, heading south. No one saw her slip off the road, but Jeremiah knew where she was going, even if he couldn't keep her pace.

Jeremiah stopped at the edge of the creek bed to catch his breath. Charlie Joe had already crossed and was racing up the path to the watermelon patch. Old Man Siley had a full garden down this way, and word was out that a family of coons was robbing his patch blind. The Gardener boys had wanted to hunt this side of the creek for years and had almost swallowed what teeth they had left in excitement when he showed up on their pappy's door step, asking if they could help him out with his little problem. Disappointment was the only thing they'd treed so far, though. Old man Siley was ready to offer a reward. He was mighty partial to his watermelons.

Jeremiah caught up with Charlie Joe at the edge of the timber. She stood behind a tree, watching the patch. A light breeze played with the edges of her hair. She stood a head taller than Jeremiah, but he didn't mind.

"It looks clear, don't it?" she asked, knowing that Old Man Siley was still in the church sanctuary when she slipped out and raced toward the timber. She had heard of the offer he had given the Gardener boys. Their family was a heathen family, so they didn't go to church. More than likely they were camped out close to the patch, watching and waiting for something to happen. Mr. Gardener was a known drunk, though, and his boys were rumored to steal a sip or two when their pappy wasn't around. If they were close, more than likely they were punch-drunk.

"I don't know, Charlie Joe. It don't feel right, stealin' watermelons on Sunday," he quietly said.

"Sissy," she taunted as she stepped away from the tree. A basketball-sized watermelon sat five yards out, in broad daylight, just begging to be picked. Charlie Joe could taste it already as she crept out into the patch. Jeremiah watched the tree line, a bad feeling welling up inside. He couldn't see anyone along the timberline, but he sensed eyes were watching them.

"Charlie Joe!" he whispered from behind the tree. "Come on! Let's get out of here!"

She ignored him as she reached down and picked the melon off the vine. A smile stretched across her pretty little face as she lifted the melon to her nose and smelled the sweetness of it. She turned and looked back at Jeremiah. She had always told him he was cute, but not very daring. He hoped she could live with that. She knew he'd do anything she asked, and she seemed to enjoy seeing him nervous. His heart beat just a bit faster whenever she was near. It's a torturous thing to be in love.

"Come get this one while I find another one!" she called.

Jeremiah could feel the sweat roll down between his shoulder blades. The late-morning sun was beating down on his conscience. He knew God saw what he was doing, and he knew for sure he was going to hell for it as he stepped out into the patch and took the melon from her hands. He loved the taste of watermelon as much as she; he just wasn't as brave. He admired Charlie's bravery as they walked back toward the timberline with their bounty, but he'd never tell her that sweet little secret.

2

Sweetwater, Missouri, Present Day

The two-story colonial home built in 1822 had a deep front porch and tall windows. James Monroe was the president of the United States when it was built, and Missouri had been added as a new state the year before with much debate. Missouri was admitted as a slave state through the Missouri Compromise. The Civil War started a month later. To say that the house had history was like saying all men have a soul. The statement was true, but did not tell the whole story. It was like telling a little white lie.

The movers had dumped most of their boxes in the large room at the front of the house. Bigger items, dressers, bed frames, and mattresses had already been carried to the bedrooms upstairs. The Petrof grand piano sat in the front room by the bay window, its moving blankets still draped over the lid. Shirley Riedel opened the front door carrying a large cardboard box full of clothes, her youngest daughter, Rachelle, tagging along behind her.

"Stuart!" she called as she dropped the heavy box on the floor by the piano and walked back toward the kitchen.

She found him under the sink, an open toolbox at his feet. Tools were strewn all around him. She could hear him quietly cussing, thinking no one was around to hear.

"Mommy, what does 'Damn!' mean?" Rachelle asked from the kitchen door. Stuart jumped, hitting his head on the pipes.

Shirley stooped down to look at him as he crawled out from under the sink.

"Yes, Daddy," she teased as she reached up and touched where he'd hit his head. "Tell Rachelle what it means."

"Very funny, Shirley," he said as he pushed her hand away and rubbed his head. She was laughing at him as he turned his back to her to get up off the floor.

"I ran down to the café and bought some dinner. Are you hungry?" she asked.

"Starving. What'd you get?" he said as he wiped his one good hand on a towel.

"Your favorite, Daddy!" Rachelle piped up as she came into the kitchen and wrapped her arms around his leg, giving him a big hug. "Mommy and I know how hard you have been working and wanted to get you something special, so we bought the works, chicken legs and 'tatoes and everything!"

Stuart laughed as he reached down to pick her up. "You bought me legs and 'tatoes!" he said, much to Rachelle's delight.

Shirley's heart swelled as she watched their exchange. He was just as handsome now as the day she married him and after almost eighteen years of marriage, she felt she was still learning the depth of his love for her.

"I'll run out to the car and get it if you and Rachelle can find some plates and silverware to use," she said as she walked back to the front door.

Stuart gave Rachelle a quick kiss on the cheek before setting her down on the floor. "Help me, girl! Mommy won't let us eat without plates!"

Rachelle giggled and raced for the first box she could get to, tearing it open and looking inside for the treasure they needed. It took them four boxes before they found one with plates, but silverware was another challenge. Shirley was back with the food before they were done looking, and Stuart wasn't going to wait for the silverware before tearing into the food.

Stuart opened the box of chicken legs when Rachelle said, "Look what I found!" She held up a zip lock bag full of spoons.

They settled on the kitchen floor eating their meal together. Stuart stretched out on his side, Shirley with her back to the kitchen cabinets.

"How's the sink coming?" she asked.

"I think I have the leak fixed," he said. "We can go ahead and unload the boxes for the kitchen today, then I think we need to take a break and check out the town—see what's going on, maybe find a church to go to tomorrow."

Shirley just smiled at him. He was such a good man—always dependable, thoughtful, good with the kids, a Christian man through and through. Stuart wasn't just a man who talked the talk. He walked what he believed and was still human enough to admit he made mistakes now and again.

"Mommy! Guess what I found today!" Rachelle said as she dropped her chicken leg and popped up off the floor and stood against the wall across the room. When she was satisfied that she had her parents' full attention, she proceeded like a magician doing a magic trick. Waving her hand over the paneling near the floor, she chanted, "Abracadabra!" and pushed against the panel, popping it open. Inside was a little cubby-hole halved by a shelf.

Rachelle stood beaming next to her discovery as Stuart and Shirley came forward to take a closer look.

"That's incredible!" Stuart said. "I wonder what it was used for."

"The real-estate agent said the house was built in the eighteen hundreds," Shirley said as she watched Rachelle climb into the space. "Since it's here in the kitchen, I suppose it could have been used as extra storage for dishes and things."

"See, Mommy? I can fit inside, and there is a little ledge here so I can pull the door closed," she said. Shirley didn't like Rachelle being inside the space. It didn't look very clean, and she thought of spiders.

"Come on out, honey," she said. "We'll clean it up a little for you, and you can put some of your dolls in there to play with when Mommy is cooking."

Excited that her mom had read her thoughts, she clamored out and secured the panel, making it completely hidden in the wall. Satisfied that her secret room was safe, she resumed her place on the floor and tucked into the chicken on her plate, a Cheshire cat smile adorning her innocent little face.

Stuart and Shirley smiled at each other, both wondering what other hidden little secrets their new home held.

"So, shall we finish eating and head out?" Stuart asked.

"Kevin and Riley are out driving around town. They should be home around five o'clock. Why don't we wait for them to come back before we go out again."

***

"This town sucks," Kevin said as he drove down Main Street in the blue '68 Mustang they shared. He sipped his pop. "There's absolutely nothing here!"

"Come on, it's not that bad," Riley said. "It's not like Chicago, but it has its advantages."

"Like what, the Dairy Cone?"

"There were some nice boys back at the Dairy Cone," Riley said. "I bet you'll make lots of friends here." She had a cheeseburger in one hand as she reached for a handful of French fries on the seat between them.

"Don't hog the fries, Riley. So far, the food is the only good thing about this day."

"Mmh," she mumbled as she raised her nose in the air and looked out her side window. "I suppose you didn't see Janet, did you?"

"Yeah, I saw her. What of it?" Kevin said.

"Did you know that she lives two blocks down from us?" Riley said. Janet had warmed up to Riley, and she suspected it was because her brother was cute. She was sure it wasn't because Janet was keen to make friends with her. It didn't fit the small-town "clique" mentality she'd heard about.

"Not interested," Kevin pronounced as he turned back toward their new home. Riley knew about his relationship with Stephanie, the girl he'd had to leave back in Chicago. The chances of that relationship surviving this move were slim to none. He appreciated Riley's attempt to help him move on, but he wasn't ready to give up that hope yet. Not yet. He pulled up to the curb outside their new home. Mom and Dad sat on the porch swing holding hands as Rachelle rode her bike up and down the sidewalk. If there was one good thing about this move, it was that they could be a family again.

3

Sweetwater, Missouri

Lance Meton had never met or seen anyone like Riley. She was beautiful, friendly, and funny. She actually looked at him and smiled when most girls shrank away from him. He smiled with the memory of her.

Lance lifted weights in his room at home, but never bulked up like the farm kids he went to school with. The Goth look he'd recently adopted didn't encourage the other kids to accept him, and that was the point. He didn't like these hicks he was forced to be around every day. Refusing to say the Pledge of Allegiance didn't win him any brownie points with the teachers either, but it was a free country, and he'd damn well do as he pleased.

He'd gone back to his car right after Kevin and Riley left the Dairy Cone so he could follow them home and find out where she lived. He parked half a block back and sat, watching them pull up to the curb outside the centennial home on Oliver Drive. Mature trees lined each side of the street, obscuring his view somewhat, but he could see a little girl riding her bike on the sidewalk. Riley walked over to her and carried her up onto the porch. Must be a little sister, he thought. That was cool. He didn't have any brothers or sisters. Family wasn't important, but he could tolerate hers if it meant he could be with her.

He sat and watched the family until they all went inside. He then turned his car around and drove back to the Dairy Cone to pick up Meretrix. A cocaine drop was scheduled for eleven thirty that night, and her services were part of the bargain. He wasn't about to miss an opportunity for sex, even for his new friend, Riley.

***

10

Stuart stood by the mailbox holding the blue envelope in his hand. He turned it over to see who had sent it. The address on the back of the envelope was printed in formal black type.

Matthew Johnson, US Marshal

Investigative Services Division

Chicago, IL

Matt had been a longtime friend of Stuart's. They went through academy together and then were assigned as Deputy US Marshals in the same division down in Virginia. Stuart had been working on the investigation involving an escaped federal prisoner when Matt had called him late in the night. His uncle Vernon was a municipal court judge in Arkansas and had been receiving death threats on a regular basis over the last couple of months. The fact that they were happening was not a big concern to Uncle Vernon, as he had experienced other impotent death threats from criminals over the years. This threat had been more concerning, though, as the message had been carried home from school in his daughter's backpack that afternoon.

Matt was denied access to the case due to family ties, so he had made a formal request to the director, asking Stuart to head the investigation. At the time of the call, Shirley was eight and a half months pregnant with twins and had been having contractions on and off for several days. Stuart was anxious to be home for the delivery, but Shirley encouraged him to go to Arkansas.

"We don't know when the babies will come, Stuart," she said. "Matt wouldn't call you unless he really needed you. And besides, my sister will be here tomorrow. You don't have to worry about us."

Stuart had gone to Arkansas and uncovered a nest of trouble. Since 2001, a Mexican drug lord named Mombasa had controlled a drug trafficking highway from the Gulf of Mexico into Cameron, Louisiana. From there, it was a straight shot up into Little Rock, Arkansas. Distribution was easy from that point until police impounded a group of semi-tractor trailers hauling over ten million dollars in crack cocaine.

A mole had given up the shipment and distribution site in Little Rock. Mombasa needed to reclaim his merchandise and clean house.

According to an unidentified yet reliable source, Spade was well known in the underworld as a man who did two things well: killing and holding a grudge. He was highly intelligent and never forgot a detail. He was a dangerous, private man looking to expand his dealings and form a business partnership. Mombasa needed Spade badly. The mole was currently tucked somewhere safely in witness protection. Judge Vernon was the key to finding his location, but he was heavily guarded as well. Spade already had a full dossier on the judge, and his family. Mombasa's job offer included a partnership in all future dealings.

Stuart's work ethic paid off quickly. Mombasa had been identified as a major player early on. Intercepting cell phone calls and encrypted emails was relatively easy. The shocking find was uncovering Spade's plans for an anthrax bomb in an apartment a block away from the judge's home. Two crates of Russian-issued AK-47 assault rifles along with other paraphernalia were found neatly organized in the apartment. Pictures of Judge Vernon, his wife, and his two daughters were pinned to the wall. Mombasa was captured and prosecuted to the full extent of the law—Spade, however, eluded police and went back underground. The police never found a fingerprint of Spade, much less a photo. He remained a ghost, and on the FBI Most Wanted list.

The untimely death of Judge Vernon occurred a few months after Mombasa's trial was over. He had been working late in his third-floor office in the Judicial Building downtown. A jury trial was on the docket to start the following day, and he had been reviewing procedures for the trial. It was late, after two a.m., when the judge was caught on the security cameras. He had paused at the top of the stairs and looked behind him for a moment. He grabbed his chest, and then for reasons unknown, tumbled backwards striking his head several times before reaching the bottom of the granite staircase. The night janitor discovered his body. He was dead by the time the ambulance arrived.

The capture and prosecution of Mombasa turned into an event that helped launch Stuart's career. It was a great ride until last year. His team had uncovered a terrorist cell in Oklahoma. During the takedown, one of his men had been hit and left in the open. Stuart, lead man on the team, extracted his man from the line of fire but not without consequences. Two upper body shots that penetrated his body armor hospitalized him for three months, six weeks of that in intensive care. Physically, his days as a US Marshal were over. His right hand still lacked the strength to hold a glass, much less a gun.

Stuart opened the blue envelope, wondering what his friend could have sent him. Inside was a card that read *Stay Out of Trouble If You Can!* along with a letter written in black ink on white parchment paper.

Dear Stuart,

> *I heard on the vine that Mombasa was paroled three weeks ago. Watch your back. If you ever get tired of being a detective for a small-town department, let me know. Until then, I'm here if you need me.*

Matt

Stuart slipped the letter and the card into the envelope as he walked back up the sidewalk to the house. He had been instrumental in putting away many criminals over the years, some of which had made parole. Once in a while a threat would come through, but nothing ever came of it and he wasn't concerned about Matt's warning. It was all just part of the job. He had a few more days to settle in before he reported in for his first day of duty. It was going to be nice to have a less stressful job. Less responsibility. Less travel. His family deserved the change, and after this last year, he was ready for it too. The fact that the man from his first real case was out of jail was unsettling, but it was unlikely that Mombasa would come for him. The mole in the Mombasa case had died a few weeks after the trial was over. It was suspected that either

Mombasa or Spade had had something to do with his untimely death, but nothing could be proven.

Shirley stepped out onto the porch as Stuart came up the walk. "Are you ready to go to the Nelsons' barbeque?" she asked. They'd met the Nelsons at church a few days prior and welcomed the opportunity to meet other townspeople at the annual back-to-school barbecue.

"Yeah, just about. Do you need help carrying anything?" he answered as he tucked the letter into the front pocket of his shirt.

"No, the twins are taking the food in their car. They'll meet us there," she said as she turned back toward the front door. "Rachelle and I will be ready in five, honey."

"Wait a minute!" Stuart protested. "You're not sending Kevin anywhere with that red velvet cake. It's my favorite, and there won't be any left by the time they get to the party!"

Riley came out the front door carrying a Tupperware bowl full of salad and a bag of chips. "Too late, Dad. The cake is spoken for, and we are rolling out to the grocery store to pick up some more pop for Mom." Kevin came out right behind her, smiling, chocolate frosting smeared on the side of his mouth.

"Now what are you eating?" Stuart demanded. Kevin acted like he didn't hear, jogging around to the driver's side of the car and jumping behind the wheel, a cupcake in each hand. The Mustang roared to life as Kevin put it in gear and pulled away from the curb.

Stuart looked down at a stray dog standing near the sidewalk. "I think I need a dog. Dogs listen when you talk. They obey. They know who's king." The dog peed on the bush at the side of the walk, then trotted away. *So much for being a big, tough guy*, Stuart thought as he walked back into the house to get his keys.

4

Sweetwater, Missouri

The Nelsons lived on Tenth Street, across from a cluster of baseball diamonds. Their house was a red brick ranch-style house with a patio and pool in the backyard. A basketball goal stood sentry in the driveway. Janet Nelson, an only child, met Shirley and Stuart in the yard and showed them back to the party.

"Are Kevin and Riley coming too?" Janet asked, taking Rachelle's hand as she ushered them around the house to where the others had gathered. Rachelle smiled up at Janet, liking the attention she was getting.

Shirley was impressed that Janet had remembered their names. Janet was good with names and faces. She never forgot a name, even if she hadn't seen someone for years. "They made a run to the store for pop, but they should be here before long."

Janet showed Shirley and Stuart to her parents, letting Rachelle go to join a group of smaller children playing at the shallow end of the pool with the water slide. She then quietly slipped away back into the front yard to wait for more guests to arrive. She had met Riley at the Dairy Cone Saturday night and really liked her. They hadn't gotten an opportunity to talk after church. Janet was hoping to get to know her better and was looking forward to seeing her again.

***

Dylan and Amy were walking across the lawn when Janet came around the corner. They were friends from school and had recently started dating.

"Hey, guys! Glad you could make it." Janet took a couple of bags of chips from Amy and said, "Everyone is out back. I hope you brought your swimsuits. The water's great!" As they were going back, Kevin and

Riley pulled up to the curb. Janet saw them pull up and turned to Amy. "You guys go on back; I'll be there in a minute."

Amy smiled and laughed as she turned to Dylan. "I have water guns, and you are going to pay for driving so fast on the way over here!" she teased.

The driveway and street were full of cars. There seemed to be a lot of people at the party already as the twins got out with an armload of food in each of their hands. Janet was by Riley almost immediately.

"Here, let me help you," she said as she took a sack of two liters from her. "I'm Janet Nelson. We met at the Dairy Cone the other night, remember?"

"Hi, Janet!" Riley said. "It's so nice to see a familiar face."

"We moved here six years ago, so I remember what it's like to be new," Janet confided. "Come with me and I'll introduce you to more of my friends." The twins followed Janet as she led them through to the backyard and the group of teenagers that had gathered over to the side.

Inside the house, Shirley was making friends with Carrie Nelson, Janet's mom, as the men congregated around the grill on the patio. They stood in the kitchen looking out the window watching as people arrived at the party.

"Janet's such a beautiful young woman, Carrie," Shirley said while mixing the salad greens and vegetables that the twins had just brought in. "You must be very proud."

People were coming into the kitchen to drop off desserts and chilled salads before heading back out to the party. Carrie said 'hi' to each of them, calling them by name and thanking them for coming before turning back to Shirley.

"Thank you. She's had a difficult couple of years but seems to have really bloomed since moving here. Janet's an only child, and her dad and I both have careers. She's been on her own a lot, I'm afraid."

"It doesn't seem to have hurt her any."

Stuart and Jim Nelson came in through the screened patio door with the meat on a platter, searching the bar area for an open spot to set it down. Carrie moved a couple of the salad bowls and rearranged the dessert area to make more room for them. Shirley caught Stuart stealing a cookie but didn't say anything, just smiled and looked away. Stuart had a horrible sweet tooth. He noticed that the red velvet cake was missing from the dessert area.

"I thought I saw the twins outside," he said as he looked out the window toward the group of teens by the pool.

"You did," Shirley assured him, laughing. She knew what he was thinking.

"Did we miss something?" Jim asked. Carrie turned and looked at Shirley to make sure that everything was OK.

"Stuart is just missing his cake, that's all," Shirley laughed. She had originally made the cake for the cookout, but since it was Stuart's favorite, she wanted to surprise him with it later. The twins had gotten a store-bought angel food cake while at the grocer to replace the one she made for Stuart, but she didn't want him to know about it yet. Carrie, not understanding, moved Janet's angel food cake from the counter to the bar area and finished arranging the food before she stepped outside to announce that everything was ready for those who were hungry.

***

"Your mom is awesome, Kevin," Dylan said as he scooped another spoonful of his mother's potato salad into his mouth, one full plate on his lap, another in his hands. Dylan played football, and putting on weight had been a goal all summer. Kevin couldn't see an ounce of fat on Dylan anywhere. His T-shirt stretched over bulging muscles. He wondered how much Dylan could bench press as he watched him scoop up another mouthful.

"She's OK," he said.

"And your sister? Gorgeous," he said as he watched Riley walk over to the edge of the pool and sit down next to a group of girls on lawn chairs. "The guys are going to be all over her as soon as school starts. She have a boyfriend?"

"No." Kevin was getting defensive, although he didn't know why. Dylan was OK. Big, pretty smart, and from what he could tell, harmless. Besides, he was dating Amy, so he was already out of the hunt as far as his sister was concerned.

"There's a group of deadheads at school you need to steer clear from," Dylan said. "One in particular. Name's Lance Meton. Bad apple if you ask me." Dylan set the empty plate on the ground next to him and picked up the full one in his lap before continuing. "I've never actually seen him do anything wrong; he just gives me the creeps."

"Why's that?" Kevin asked.

"Dude's always alone, except when you see him out at night after a football game or at a postgame bonfire. Then it's usually some older guys who don't go to school here. In fact, I don't really think they are from around here. Dresses weird. Funky hair. Know what I mean?"

Kevin wasn't sure how to take Dylan. Funky clothes to a farm boy could mean that you are wearing your pliers on the wrong hip, or your cowboy hat is brown instead of black. He smiled at the thought. One man's definition of weird could be another man's definition of art. Discernment was going to be a necessity to survive here. He'd make his own decisions about the people he met and try to keep what he heard from defining his first impressions. That didn't mean he wasn't going to keep an eye out for this guy, though.

"What's his name again?"

"Lance Meton. Can't miss him. Wears black all the time. Tattoo on his left arm of some big dragon with wings or something. Keeps it covered up most of the time, except when it's really hot. Don't rightly know about his parents. Never seen them. Hey, you try this chicken yet? It's good!"

"I'm going back in for more. You want anything?" Kevin stood up to go into the house. He wanted to circulate some more and meet some other kids before heading out.

"Nah, I'm good for now," he said. "Amy gets mad at me if I get seconds."

***

Janet was sitting at the edge of the pool next to Riley, their feet in the water. Riley hadn't brought a swimming suit, so she stayed on the edge of the pool as Janet slipped into the cool blue water and swam to the other side to visit with Amy. Riley noticed what a good swimmer Janet was and envied her. She'd never liked the water and didn't know how to swim. She could float for a little while, in an emergency, if she kept herself calm, but that was a big if. On the whole, Riley didn't really go in for sports. Making friends had always been difficult for her because she was so shy—until she sat down at the piano. Touching the ivory keys transformed her into something else: a bold, passionate woman who could express deep emotions from the soundless notes on a piece of music. She hadn't played for weeks, and she was missing it like an old friend.

Janet had told her that Jordan High School had an art department, but their art teacher had resigned at the end of last year, and she didn't know who had been hired to replace her. Apparently, because of budget cuts, the art department and the music department had been combined three years earlier, so the loss of the art teacher meant that the music programs were all on hold as well. This was a huge discouragement for Riley, but she decided to keep her hopes up and make the best of whatever situation she found when school started next week. Besides, she thought, I don't have to play the piano at school.

The idea of it all depressed her despite her attempts to remain cheerful. *Lord, I can't give up my music. I've left my friends and the huge music department at my old school already. This town is so small compared to where we lived before, and I'm not good at making friends. Kevin is having a hard time adjusting; I can see it in him. We both want Mom and Dad to be happy, but really, this may be asking too much. Somehow, please, help us find our rhythm here. Help me be the person you want me to be.*

"Hey, Riley! Come help us set up the volleyball net," Amy shouted. The girls had gotten out of the pool and were headed toward the garage while Riley had been lost in her thoughts. She got up to join them.

"I've never played volleyball before," she said to herself with a groan. "This should be interesting."

5

Blackhorse, Missouri

"This is a piece of crap, Arnold, and you know it!" she yelled as she threw the papers back at him.

"Watch your language, Charlie Joe," he warned. "I know it's not what you expected, but Audrey Lemoine is going to have to stand in front of Judge Winkler on Friday in order to get her kids back." Arnold Dory wiped the sweat beading up on his forehead. It was still pretty warm in Missouri this time of year, but it wasn't the weather that was making him sweat. He'd grown up in the same town as Charlie Joe and had a crush on her all through high school. Charlie Joe was known to have what some called a "difficult" personality. Her momma had tried to rein in Charlie's strong-willed nature, but try as she did, God rest her soul, Charlie Joe usually got her way. It didn't help that the woman was damn smart too.

"Audrey would wet her pants if she knew she had to stand in front of Judge Winkey on Friday," Charlie Joe threw back at him. Arnold winced at the nickname she had attached to the judge. "The poor woman doesn't stand a chance, Arnold!"

"First of all, you'll be there with her. Secondly, don't call the judge 'Winkey.' It's disrespectful." Arnold stood up from his leather office chair and came around the mahogany desk to stand in front of Charlie Joe. It was a weak attempt to show authority, but it was an attempt nonetheless. Charlie Joe stood a head taller than Arnold. She looked down at him as she tried to hide a grin. She knew what he was up to, and she would beat him at this game. Arnold Dory was Audrey's court-appointed attorney, and he hadn't done an honest day's work his entire life. His money was inherited, not something he earned. Confrontation was a beast that terrified Arnold Dory. It was a character flaw that did not bode well in his profession.

"Listen, Charlie Joe," he said as he tried to calm himself. She always got him riled up, and he didn't know how she did it. "Neil Lemoine is the pappy to those kids, and he has just as much right to them as she does. Granted, his drinking does weigh in her favor, but she's going to have to show up in court and prove to the judge that she deserves to have sole custody, if that's what she wants. Otherwise, and this is a worst-case scenario, the judge will have them split the week. Alternating two days at Mom's house, two days with Dad." A drop of sweat slid down his cheek as he stood in front of her.

She didn't blink, just stood there in front of Arnold, silent. One beat, two beats. Arnold didn't know what to do or say. "Well, I guess since you're her lawyer, you'd know best about these things, seeing how you know the law and everything." Charlie Joe stepped back and then stopped. "But seeing how she's my best friend, and I'm speaking in her stead, I'd say you better be on time to court on Friday." She smiled through gritted teeth as she turned and walked away.

"Charlie Joe! Don't you be pulling any of your antics in court!" he feebly warned. The problem with her was loyalty. If Charlie Joe decided she liked you, she'd cut her own heart out to make sure you were safe and cared for; but if she didn't like you, well, God help you. Arnold shook his head as he turned back to his desk and all the paperwork that awaited him there. He dreaded Friday.

***

Charlie Joe Bingham was seething as she marched across the street from the Dory Law Office to Big Daddy's Diner. Cora Mae Vaxter was working the counter as usual and saw her come in the door. The place was nearly empty except for the lingering coffee drinkers gathered in the corner to gossip and read the local paper. Charlie Joe's ears were always red when she was mad, and Cora Mae could see by the glow that this was going to be a loud conversation as she quickstepped it to the front counter.

"Back here, CJ," she said, motioning as she led her into the kitchen. "Spill it," she commanded. Charlie Joe, Cora Mae, and Audrey had been best friends all through school. Audrey had been the only one to take the dreaded walk down the aisle of doom. They had all stayed close after high school, so Cora Mae was well aware of Audrey's predicament.

"Judge Winkler comes in here every Monday afternoon for pie." It was a statement, not a question, and Cora Mae didn't know what to make of it.

"What, you want me to poison him?" She laughed, attempting to use humor to calm Charlie Joe.

"Well, hell, I hadn't thought of that," Charlie Joe said as she leaned against the wall. The sink was full of dirty dishes, and the floor was sticky, but the smells coming from the grill made her stomach rumble. She'd missed breakfast, and it was well past lunchtime. Eddie Morton Jr. was the owner of Big Daddy's Diner and was manning the grill at the moment. He also was Cora Mae's boyfriend, but that wasn't common knowledge around town; at least they didn't know it was. He saw them come into the kitchen and brought two barstools over for them to sit on, along with a couple of grilled turkey sandwiches. Charlie Joe wondered whose order she was eating but didn't look a gift horse in the mouth as she tucked into the food.

"I need a favor, Cora Mae. What are you doin' Friday at one o'clock?" she asked between bites.

Whatever Charlie Joe was up to was going to be good, and Cora Mae wasn't about to miss it. "Eddie, I need Friday afternoon off!" she announced as she looked at Charlie Joe. "I've got some personal business to attend to."

***

Arnold Dory had the largest bank account in the county, but he only owned two suits; one for weddings and funerals, the other for court. His hair was thinning on top, and in keeping with family tradition, he opted for the comb-over look in a vain attempt to cling to an appearance of youth. His knees knocked together when he walked, and the fact that he was pigeon-toed exaggerated the slow, lumbering manner in which he moved. It was ten minutes until one, and Judge Winkler was not a man who tolerated lateness in his court. Arnold wiped the sweat from his forehead as he watched Audrey's yellow Chevy truck pull into a parking space near the front of the courthouse. Charlie Joe and Cora Mae piled out of the passenger's side, each with a large box in their hands. Charlie Joe led the parade up the courthouse steps, walking past Arnold as they made their way into the courtroom.

Neil Lemoine and his lawyer were already seated. The children sat in the back of the courtroom with Audrey's parents. Besides the bailiff and the court reporter, no one else was present in the courtroom. Charlie Joe sat the boxes down on the table and took a seat next to Audrey. Cora Mae sat behind them and watched as Arnold took notice of what was going on.

"Charlie Joe, I think you'd best have a seat next to Cora Mae," he said.

"Tell him, Audrey," Charlie Joe said.

"Have a seat, Arnold. Charlie Joe isn't going anywhere," Audrey said resolutely. Arnold was surprised and not just a little worried.

Court was called to session as Judge Winkler entered the room. They sat and waited as he looked over this docket, then out at the faces in his courtroom.

"Says here that this is Case Number SG08D-000523. A matter of custody between the plaintiff, Audrey Lemoine, and the defendant, Neil Lemoine, is to be decided today. It says that Audrey wants sole custody of her two children. Mr. Dory, are you counsel for the plaintiff?"

"Yes sir, I am." Arnold stood while he addressed the judge.

"Please state your case." The judge took his spectacles off as he leaned back in his chair.

"If I may, sir." Charlie Joe stood and began opening the box in front of her.

Judge Winkler leaned forward and squinted his eyes. "Charlie Joe, what are you doing in my courtroom?"

"As requested by my friend Audrey here, and with the permission of Mr. Dory, I'm presenting the case, sir," she confidently said. Arnold was afraid to admit he didn't know what was going on. Charlie Joe had attended college at Washburn University, then after graduating from law school at Kansas University, she passed the bar exam for both Missouri and Kansas. CJ was more than qualified to appear in court; she just had never had a reason to practice law since passing the bar exam.

"Is this true, Mr. Dory?"

"Yes sir," he said. Sweat dripped off his back into his underwear. He took a legal pad out of his briefcase and made like he was going to pass information on to Audrey in an attempt to look important. His stomach roiled and it was sheer determination that prevented a gastric event from occurring in his pants. Arnold Dory did not handle stress well.

"What do you have in the box, Charlie Joe?" the judge asked.

"Well, I have a bit of a problem, sir. I have an entire chocolate peanut butter pie with graham cracker crust sitting here," she said as she peeked down into the box. "Looks like there is a meringue toppin' on it with chocolate sprinkles. Can't rightly say that I've ever had this *specific* type of pie, but it sure looks good enough to eat, and in this heat, I'm afraid it's going to spoil real soon." A look of worry and regret was plastered across her face as she looked up at the judge. "Would you like a piece?"

"Are you attempting to buy my favors, Charlie Joe?" the judge questioned.

"No sir! I would *never* do such a thing. I just thought you'd like to share some pie while I lay this case before you; but if you'd rather not..."

She let the statement die away while she slowly began to close the lid to the box.

The judge gave an audible sigh. "Do the defendant and his lawyer have any objections to eating pie?" he asked.

Enix Black, lawyer for Neil Lemoine, stood. "No sir, so long as a piece makes its way to this side of the courtroom."

Charlie Joe passed the pie back to Cora Mae to be cut and passed around as she reached for the second box and placed it on top of the table. She opened the box and began to place its contents on the table, pausing to wait until the judge had his pie before she began. The court reporter put her slice on the floor next to her as there was no room on her little side table to hold it. The judge eagerly took his first bite as Charlie Joe began.

"Your Honor, do you believe in evolution?" she asked. Without waiting for an answer, she continued. "I believe our country is going to hell in a hand basket because we no longer honor God—you know, the same God who gave us the Ten Commandments. Remember, in 2004 the Honorable Roy Moore in Alabama was removed from his bench because he did not adhere to a federal order to remove these sacred documents from the rotunda of a judicial building. Have you seen the state of Alabama recently, Your Honor? Let me remind you that on August 29, 2005, Hurricane Katrina touched the state of Alabama; the shores still bear the scars.

"Now, I wouldn't presume to know the mind of God, nor elude that Katrina was an act of judgment. I merely remind the court that there are always consequences to every action. Take, for instance, the pie that you're eating." Charlie Joe paused a moment, then stepped out from behind the desk. "I have placed all the ingredients, save one, the secret ingredient, on this desk behind me. If you believe the religion of evolution, or better yet, the religion of the big bang theory, you would hold that these ingredients would randomly come together, bake, and become the pie that you are eating now. In the case of evolution, the peanuts and the cocoa beans would evolve into that same pie."

Enix Black, with chocolate pie at the corner of his mouth, stood. "Your Honor, as entertaining as this may be, we are here to discuss a matter of custody, not religion and pie."

Charlie Joe was quick to retort. "If it pleases Your Honor, I will quickly get to the point."

"Proceed."

"Everyone in this courtroom knows that you, Your Honor, are a fine Christian man. I believe we agree that the pie you are eating did not evolve. It was created." Charlie Joe paused as she walked over to the defendant's table before continuing. "I ask you this. Can a violent man like Neil Lemoine evolve into a polished, mild-mannered gentleman; or will he remain who he is and continue beating his family to the point of death?"

"Your Honor, I have to object." Enix Black chuckled as he spoke. "There is no evidence of abuse here."

"I have proof, Your Honor, that Audrey Lemoine has suffered at the defendant's hand and that to allow the children to have unsupervised visitation with their father would not only endanger their health, but their very lives," she pronounced. "Would it be right to subject them to such dangers?"

"I know of no such evidence, Your Honor!" Enix Black was on his feet. Neil Lemoine uncrossed his legs and turned so that he faced Audrey Lemoine. He stared at her from across the room, clenching and unclenching his fists.

"Approach the bench," Judge Winkler commanded as he wiped his face. "You too, Mr. Dory."

Arnold Dory felt a pain in his chest as he heaved his huge body up out of the narrow wooden chair and lumbered toward the bench. His mind was racing, searching for some hint as to what Charlie Joe might be up to this time. A plumb line of sweat streaked down his back from his shoulder blades to the beltline of his pants as he stood with the others, looking up at Judge Winkler.

The judge's glasses were perched at the end of his nose as he looked directly down at Charlie Joe. He'd known her since she was first brought to the courthouse as an infant. He knew about her background even though it was a closed adoption proceeding. He had met her biological parents. They had been young, and unmarried at the time the adoption went through his circuit court. Her adoptive parents, Mr. and Mrs. Bingham, had tried for years to have children, but Dr. Jones had never been optimistic. In the end he convinced them that adoption was the only alternative, and with Judge Winkler's help through an old classmate from law school, a healthy little girl became the joy and purpose of life for Mr. and Mrs. Bingham. He'd caught a lot of flak for allowing a black couple to adopt a white baby, and against his better judgment, he stood firm against the racial tide and pushed to make it happen. More than once the town had been on the verge of a civil war for various other reasons, but somehow the fact that the Bingham family existed within their mists calmed those deep waters. So much, in fact, that the Bingham's had been invited to join the white Baptist church in town. Both Baptist churches were struggling to meet their bills, and the Bingham's felt that if they accepted the invitation, it would open the door to combining the two churches, solving many of the financial problems both struggled to overcome. Judge Winkler knew that the white folks had an ulterior motive: to keep an eye on how Charlie Joe was being treated, but the outcome of that collective community decision was that a racial divide had been crossed. Trust had developed. Friendships had formed and a community had begun to change for the better.

"Charlie Joe," the judge said. "Please tell me that this isn't some prank you've come up."

"No sir!" she loudly exclaimed. "I have proof that Mr. Lemoine—"

"What lies did you tell 'em, Audrey?" Neil shouted as he jumped up from his chair and rushed at her from across the room.

Audrey, shocked at Neil's outburst in the courtroom, shrank back, unable to rise from her chair before he shoved Cora Mae aside, grabbing Audrey by the front of her dress, then lifting her to her feet. Fear and rage were etched across his sober face, and he shouted, "What'd you say, woman! Tell me right now!"

The bailiff closed a handcuff on Neil Lemoine's left wrist and pulled his arm behind his back to subdue him. Neil's instant rage continued as the bailiff struggled to pull him back.

"Order in the court," Judge Winkler shouted as he pounded his gavel. The court reporter shot out of the courtroom to call for help as Neil broke free from the bailiff and lunged after Charlie Joe.

"You bitch!" he shouted at Charlie Joe. "I'll kill you for this!"

Two large men in uniform appeared suddenly and pinned the screaming Neil Lemoine to the floor at Charlie Joe's feet. Flushed, Charlie Joe turned back to the judge. Cora Mae and Audrey cowered on the floor under the window of the courtroom, taking it all in. She could hear the children in the back crying and worried.

"You see, Your Honor? He is not a man who can control his emotions, and as vividly displayed before your court, he is also a man prone to violence. What further proof do you need that he is unfit to have custody of these children?"

"Bailiff, remove this man from my courtroom," the judge ordered. "Mr. Black, I do not tolerate violence in my courtroom. Thus, I am giving temporary sole custody of these children to their mother. Your client has six months of anger management therapy to be completed at the community health department with Dr. Hicks. If he fails to appear for more than two sessions in six months, he loses permanent custody of his children. At the end of six months, he will reappear in this courtroom, with Dr. Hicks, to determine whether or not partial custody is appropriate. In the meantime, he may have supervised visitations at the SRS building twice a week for one hour. Also, he will undergo drug and alcohol testing twice a month. If he comes up positive, therapy will be extended in a manner appropriate to the findings. If I find that he harasses Mrs. Lemoine or Miss Charlie Joe Bingham in any manner, he will be placed in custody until I feel he has learned that threatening a woman is not appropriate. That may be a very long time, Mr. Black. I advise you to be sure your client fully understands my decision."

"Yes sir, Your Honor," Mr. Black said.

"Mr. Dory and Charlie Joe? In my chambers. Now!" The judge rose from his bench and with his black robes flowing, left the room.

Arnold Dory's hands were shaking as he looked from Enix Black back to Charlie Joe. He couldn't believe what had just happened. He took a deep breath and turned toward the judge's chambers. Charlie Joe straightened her powder-blue two-piece suit and followed Arnold. She closed the door behind her as she entered the chamber. Judge Winkler was removing his robes and hanging them in the closet used to store them. He was a meticulous man. Smart, observant, and read people well- skills that served him well during his lean lawyer years before he was appointed judge thirty-five years earlier. Those same skills hadn't diminished over the years, and he used them now as he observed the two people standing before him.

"Mr. Dory, did you have any idea what was going to happen in my courtroom today?" he asked.

"No sir, I admit that I did not," Arnold quietly responded. He was afraid that he was going to be fined, or worse, locked up in the county jail for a few days.

Frowning, Judge Winkler sat down in his overstuffed leather desk chair and folded his hands in front of him. "I have not been impressed with you over the years, Mr. Dory," the judge began. "But you did have the foresight to allow Miss Bingham to be part of the proceedings, even though she has no practical experience in the courtroom. She saved your case today, despite the courtroom antics displayed."

Mr. Dorey nodded, without looking up. Charlie Joe, however, never took her eyes off the judge. She stood there, defiant and proud. The judge turned his attention to her.

"Miss Bingham," he began. Her chin rose an inch at the mention of her name. "You first entered my court as an infant for an adoption proceeding. That was a proud moment in my career. The only other time I found you here was after you and Jeremiah Stone were caught stealing watermelons."

"And if you remember correctly, Your Honor," she said, "I provided evidence that day that Old Man Stecher was growing marijuana next to Mr. Siley's patch of watermelons, which eventually led to one of the largest drug busts in this county. That information was a major coup for you, sir, and bolstered your campaign the following year."

***

Judge Winkler stifled a smile. He admired Charlie Joe. She was quick on her feet and always ready for whatever life threw at her. He leaned back in his chair, watching her. She had grown into a beautiful single woman, and if he were thirty years younger, he would have made a run to marry her.

"You still living in the home your parents left for you, Charlie Joe?" he asked.

"Yes sir," she replied. "Plan to till the day I die."

"What other plans do you have for your life?"

"I'm not sure I know what you mean, Your Honor."

"You're good with people, Charlie Joe. Ever think about working in the judicial system full time?" he asked.

Caught off guard, she looked at Arnold for guidance. He was a blank wall in the guidance department. She looked back at the judge but didn't answer. Charlie Joe had learned to cook from her momma, and when she had a mind to, she could fix a Southern meal that would cause men to fight for seconds. She played the piano as well, and as it pleased her, she would wander into the foyer of the Marque Hotel downtown and play for hours on end; then suddenly, as if remembering she left tea on the stove, she'd up and leave without so much as a "how do you do." She didn't have a formal job and wasn't sure she cared to have one. She had a law degree from Kansas University but hadn't had reason to use it until today. Money was never an issue for Charlie Joe. Her pappy had been a saver, and when he passed, he left her a home free and clear, with an investment portfolio rivaled only by the banker over in Mayetteville. She had a few nice things, things that meant something to her. But beyond that, she didn't go in for pretentiousness and often as not, wore secondhand clothes bought at a shop in the next town over and hand-me-downs her friends were tossing out.

Judge Winkler knew what was running through her mind. Charlie Joe was strong willed and independent, and the judge was of the mind that women of this variety only needed a good husband and a few kids to settle them down. Jeremiah Stone had grown into a fine man and a good sheriff. For the life of him, he couldn't understand why they had never gotten married. This might be the perfect opportunity and at his age, the thought of playing matchmaker entertained him some.

"You played Mr. Lemoine in that courtroom, Charlie Joe. It was a smart move, but not one without consequences. I'm going to give you a choice: either you go to jail for thirty days, or you work with the district attorney's office doing pro bono cases. You're a damn good lawyer, Charlie Joe. It's a shame you have such a quick mind and you're not using it. I don't doubt that your momma would want to see you helping those less fortunate in this world, while the opportunity presents itself. What's it going to be?"

"How long do I have to decide?" she asked. She knew very well what Judge Winkler was about. Either choice put her in the cross hairs of Sheriff Jeremiah Stone. The remodeling of the judicial buildings had forced the DA's office to be placed in the same building as the sheriff's department. Working with the DA doing pro bono cases essentially meant that she would be spending the better part of her days within feet of Sheriff Stone. It was no secret that Sheriff Stone had his heart set on winning her over, but she wasn't one to have others play her hand for her. Forcing her to spend time with the sheriff was the agenda; her voice in the courtroom today only offered the judge the vehicle to advance it, and it angered her that he was taking the opportunity to do just that.

"You have one hour. Otherwise, you're going to jail."

***

Charlie Joe was fuming when she and Arnold exited the judge's chambers. Her ears were flaming red, and her strides were confined to the boundaries of the tight powder-blue suit she wore. She couldn't wait to get out of those clothes and back into her jeans and boots, but there was war to wage before she retreated back home. Arnold was careful to stay out of her line of sight and quietly pulled away to exit the courthouse via the back door. He had just narrowly escaped a bad situation and wasn't about to tango with a wildcat like Charlie Joe. Audrey Lemoine was standing just outside the courtroom with Cora Mae when they saw Charlie Joe and Arnold exit the chambers. She scurried after CJ down the front of the courthouse steps. It was early afternoon yet, and a gentle breeze was playing in the leaves of the maple trees in the park across the street.

"CJ!" Audrey called, but Charlie Joe didn't slow and made no move to acknowledge that Audrey was trying to get her attention. Instead, she increased her stride, making a beeline for the sheriff's department in the adjacent building.

6

Sweetwater, Missouri

It was early Monday morning, and Shirley was sitting at the kitchen table still in her housecoat drinking coffee, looking through a small decorative cardboard box that she had saved over the years. It was small, only holding a few items that for Shirley held sentimental value beyond words. Pictures of her at various stages of her first pregnancy. A sonogram showing the sex of the baby. A clipping of her baby's hair after she was born, tied with a little pink ribbon. Inked footprints taken while they were still at the hospital. Stuart knew she had the box, but rarely looked at it. He encouraged her to keep it, but told her to never share it with the other kids. It was his one unbending rule, and Shirley, especially today, needed to share it with someone. It was the birthday of their firstborn, a little girl given up for adoption. Each year, on her birthday, Shirley would write her daughter a love letter. It was therapeutic for Shirley and some day maybe, she might get the chance to share these letters with her. It was a hope she had clung to since the day she gave her up for adoption. Despite the deep sorrow she felt, she would honor Stuart's one wish; she would never go against him in this, although it pained her. She drank the dark coffee as she ran her slim fingers over the inking, wondering what had happened to her, if she was happy. A sadness began to well up inside Shirley, and as footsteps carried down the hallway, she quietly closed the lid to the box and temporarily hid it on a shelf, behind some old, rarely used cookbooks. Locking the sadness back deep inside, she put on a smile and turned toward the approaching footsteps. She would write her letter later, when the children were asleep, and put the box back into the safe in the home office.

Rachelle stood in the doorway still in lavender footy pajamas, watching her. "Mommy, I'm hungry," she whined in her tiny voice as she rubbed her eyes. Bear, a favorite stuffed toy, dangled at her side.

The first day of school started in a few hours, and Rachelle would be attending first grade, a difficult step for both of them. Shirley walked over to her and picked her up.

"How about some bacon and toast? Does that sound good, sweetheart?" she said as she walked back toward the stove. Kevin and Riley would be getting up soon too, and the smell of bacon always helped pull the twins from their beds. Teenagers and their insatiable need for sleep never ceased to amaze her. Rachelle laid her head upon Shirley's shoulder in quiet reply as Shirley turned up the gas on the top and reached for the bacon in the refrigerator. Stuart walked into the room, handsome as ever in khaki pants, with a pale-blue shirt and dark-blue tie. He smiled at Shirley and Rachelle as he poured a cup of coffee.

"Ready for a big day, Munchkin?" he grinned. Rachelle loved his nickname for her and giggled quietly but didn't reply further. Shirley put her down, and she made it over to the table and sat down next to her daddy as he opened up the paper.

"Anything exciting going on in the world today, Shirley?" he asked. She was a morning person and always had the coffee ready and the paper read before Stuart's feet hit the floor.

"Nothing unusual today," she said as she turned the bacon and began pouring milk for Rachelle. "A good day for everyone to start fresh," she encouraged. She knew that Stuart felt this job was a step down for him, and he struggled with it emotionally. The pay wasn't that much different, but the status was significantly lower in his eyes. That, coupled with the injury, was making it a hard adjustment for him, but he was working hard to stay positive. He didn't expect to ever regain full use of his hand, but he was becoming more comfortable using his left hand. Shooting a gun again would be another matter, though.

"No breakfast for me today, hon," he said as he closed the paper and gulped the coffee. "I'm meeting Will Langdon and Hank Lawson over at the cafe this morning for breakfast before work." Stuart stood and put his mug in the sink, then turned and kissed her. Before heading out the door, he kissed Rachelle on the top of her head and grabbed his coat. Smiling, he turned back and looked at Shirley. "Wish me luck!" he said as he closed the door behind him.

Shirley laughed, knowing he didn't need any. The police department of this small town was ecstatic to land a man of Stuart's experience and credentials. Whatever he did, he gave it his best, and luck had very little to do with it.

She finished frying the bacon and made toast for Rachelle. Shirley left her at the table and began getting ready to take her to school when she heard Riley come down the stairs.

"Make sure Kevin gets up too, will you, Riley?" she asked. "I don't want either of you late on your first day."

Riley made for the coffeepot. "Yeah, yeah, whatever," she replied as she poured a cup and started back up the staircase. Riley hated mornings, and it was always with trepidation that anyone spoke to her before she had coffee. Shirley gave her room and didn't push the subject. Trust was something freely offered in the Riedel home, and something no one took for granted.

***

Milton's Cafe sat just off the main highway leading into Sweetwater, Missouri. Chuck Milton, who had inherited it from his uncle ten years ago, owned it. Chuck had painted the interior a cheery yellow and put new booths in along the north end. The bar of the cafe retained its original Formica and stools, giving it a nostalgic air. The floor retained its original tile, and areas that were chipped or broken had been replaced with new tile that was a close match, but upon close inspection could be identified as new. Overall, it was a clean and friendly atmosphere that Stuart walked in to that early Monday morning. Hank Lawson was first to see Stuart walk through the door and stood up from his place at a nearby table to greet him.

"You must be Stuart Riedel, our new detective," he said as he gave Stuart a firm handshake, instantly noticing Stuart's weakened hand in the greeting. "Come on over and sit down." Will Langdon was working over a cup of black coffee and put his cup down before extending his own invitation.

"Stuart, good to see you again!" Will said. "Have a seat. Are ya hungry?"

A waitress came over and took their orders and poured coffee for the threesome as pleasantries were exchanged. Stuart had met Sheriff Will Langdon a few months back during his formal interview but had not met Deputy Hank Lawson before. Hank had dreaded Stuart's arrival on the small force and had given serious thought to resigning if Will really went through with hiring an ex-US marshal. After meeting Stuart, or more honestly, after seeing he had a disability, he was much more welcoming toward this new man on the team.

"After we eat, we'll go on over to the office and show you around," Sheriff Langdon offered. "I think this week we'll just plan on you getting the lay of the land and settling in—give you a chance to get some history on our town and its people before you dive into our caseload."

"Sounds great, Sheriff," Stuart agreed.

"Just call me Will. Everyone else does 'round here. You'll find we're pretty informal and quite a friendly group. You might meet some resistance with some of the townsfolk at first. We don't have a lot of newcomers here, but once they get to know you, they'll warm up and treat you like family."

After eating breakfast Hank took the squad car while Sheriff Langdon rode with Stuart in his car over to the western edge of town. The sheriff's office resided at a diagonal from the post office and the library. The grade school was one block over, and as Stuart passed, he briefly wondered how Rachelle was doing on her first day of school.

"Hank has had some trouble getting used to you joining us here in town, Stuart," Sheriff Langdon began as they parked in front of the sheriff's office. "Don't take anything he says or does too seriously at first. He'll need some time to get used to you. He's a good cop, just doesn't like change, is all."

Stuart just smiled as he looked over the front of the building. He knew better. Hank felt threatened by him, and he sensed that somehow, the weakness in his right hand had demeaned him in Hank's eyes. It wasn't uncommon, Stuart was learning, for a man to be judged by outward weaknesses, especially in the field of law enforcement.

"You have those three files ready for me, Sheriff?" he asked. "I'll settle in faster with a caseload to focus on."

"Thought I'd give you a few days to settle in first, but if you'd rather just jump into it, I have them locked in my office, Stuart. I have to ask you, son, what happened up in Chicago? Oh, I know you were shot and that it almost killed you, but what happened?" It had been on his mind since the interview, but he wanted to wait until Stuart was moved in and on the job before he questioned him about his injury.

Stuart knew what he was asking. What happened in those moments before shots were fired? Did he flinch? Was he slow? Did he set up the takedown and miss a detail? It was an honest question pregnant with inferred overtones. What Sheriff Langdon was really asking was if Stuart could be trusted in the fire.

Stuart turned and looked at him, full in the face, before he answered. "I believe that deep down, there is good in everyone, and if given the chance, most people will try to do what's right. Some people disappoint you, though, and would choose to kill you rather than accept any help you might offer them. What happened in Chicago wasn't a mistake, Sheriff. The takedown went exactly as planned. I got shot, and now I'm here. End of story."

To his credit Sheriff Will Langdon let the matter drop and got out of the car. Stuart followed him to the door, where the sheriff turned and faced him.

"My wife makes a mean brisket, Stuart. You bring your wife over Saturday night for dinner," he said with a smile. "I heard a rumor that you're mighty partial to red velvet cake too." He chuckled as he turned to open the door.

Small towns. You didn't have to be in one long before your name was connected to the rumor mill. This certainly wasn't anything new to him or Shirley. They'd both grown up in a small town, but that certainly didn't make dealing with it any easier.

***

Jordan High School was a large brick freestanding building on the south end of town. A breezeway connected the gymnasium to the main body of the school, and two outlying buildings were used for shop classes. The football field lay to the south of the school itself, and an uncut cornfield lay just beyond it.

The last bell of the day had rung as kids began filling the halls and making their ways to their respective after-school activities.

Lance Meton had skipped his last class to position himself to bump into Riley coming out of her composition class. He had it planned and mentally had executed it a hundred times over the last two days. He would act surprised, help her pick up her books, and offer her a ride home. What he hadn't expected was Janet Nelson attaching herself to Riley and keeping her attention so diverted from him. The hallway filled up, and before he knew it, Riley had slipped past him and was headed toward the front door instead of her locker.

"Seriously, Janet! Go home and get that piece, and I'll help you with it tonight," she said to her new friend as they walked to Janet's car.

"The tryouts for the play are in one week, Riley! I can't possibly have it ready to perform by then." Janet had secretly hoped that Riley would help her, but the thought of actually performing instead of just dreaming about it frightened her just a little.

Riley laughed. "Janet. You can't succeed if you don't try. I'll be home in an hour. Get your piece, and I'll meet you there. I have to go back to my locker and get my science homework. Promise me you'll be at my house in an hour." Riley wasn't going to take no for an answer.

"OK, if you're sure," Janet said.

"I'm sure, Janet." She smiled as she turned back toward the school.

Riley walked up to the front doors and reached to open it when Lance Meton suddenly appeared.

"Hey, Riley!" he said as he gave his most charming smile. "Need a ride home?"

"Thanks, Lance, but I drove the Mustang today and am meeting Janet in a little while. I appreciate the offer, though." She slid past him into the foyer.

"Maybe some other time then," Lance said as Riley turned to smile at him before continuing into the school. She didn't say yes, but she didn't refuse either. On the whole, it was a bit of a coup for Lance. He'd have to find a more creative way to get her attention, but at least she was talking to him, he thought as he headed out toward the parking lot. He knew that planning and patience were his allies in reaching his goals. Without them disaster was sure to happen, and anything less than success was not acceptable. He would have Riley. It was just a matter of when he would have her and for how long.

7

Blackhorse, Missouri

Jeremiah Stone sat at his desk in the sheriff's office looking at his list of open cases. There had been a spray-painting incident in the schoolyard recently, two burglaries, and a stolen tractor in the last week. Mr. Stecher's bull got out and did some damage to Mrs. Henson's sweet corn patch, but after talking to the two parties individually, he believed that Mrs. Henson would drop the charges against Mr. Stecher in lieu of payment for damages. Although his mind skimmed over the individual cases, he was really thinking on Charlie Joe.

He'd been in love with her since grade school, when he had spent more time in detention because of her than he cared to admit. Charlie Joe had never backed down from a challenge and somehow always landed on her feet even in the most dire circumstances. He smiled as he remembered the time Audrey Jensen (now Lemoine) overheard her father say he was going to drown a litter of pups her dog had given birth to three weeks earlier. CJ got wind of it and snuck out of the house late that night, then ran the two miles to Jeremiah's house to wake him. Faces smeared black with soot from her pappy's wood stove, they took his mare, Babe, and rode to Audrey's house with two empty gunnysacks in a covert rescue to rival a military operation.

The problem was, Audrey had heard wrong, and when her daddy saw the puppies missing a few hours later, all hell broke loose. Who knew that Audrey's dog was a national prizewinning hound dog worth thousands- of dollars? And those puppies? All but one of the puppies had been sold. He and CJ had only "saved" the puppies for a few hours before Audrey broke down and told her daddy what had happened. Two of the sheriff's deputies had been scouring the area in search of the litter when they got the call that they were being hidden in CJ's tree house on her pappy's back forty. CJ, still thinking that Audrey's daddy was going to drown the puppies, had holed up with a BB gun and held

41

the "killers" off for two hours, until the sheriff arrived with Audrey and her daddy in tow. By then CJ's pappy, Jeremiah, and his daddy had arrived. Seemed like the whole town knew what had happened before CJ lowered the puppies down and relinquished them back to their rightful owner. Instead of discipline, CJ found herself on the front page of the local paper for her determination and bravery.

The memory of those puppies still touched him. Even now he was discovering new depths of CJ's personality. CJ had quit talking to him a few weeks ago when he had asked her to marry him, for the third time. Cora Mae kept him abreast of her doings, though, so he was well aware that she had been spending a lot of time over at the law library in Hampton, Missouri, preparing for Audrey Lemoine's case today. Cora Mae was to call him and let him know how things turned out as soon as court was adjourned. His main problem right now was how to win CJ's heart once and for all. She was a stubborn woman, but then he'd known that about her his whole life. Giving up on marrying CJ just wasn't in the cards for Jeremiah Stone. She was his first, and only love.

He leaned back in his wooden office chair and took stock of his office as he considered his plight. Sometimes it seemed a painful and complicated process to find the love of your life in grade school. He knew more about CJ than he did his own little sister.

Jordan Morey opened the door to the sheriff's office. "Boss, trouble's coming from across the street."

Jeremiah walked over to the window and peeked through the blind in time to see CJ charging across the street. Even from this distance, he could see her ears were red.

"Oh shit." He needed to clear out the office before she hit the door. He'd known there was something big going on over at the courthouse when Festus had brought Neil Lemoine over to the jail. Whatever brought CJ this way had to be huge, and by the looks of things, it wasn't something she was happy about.

"Jordan, get Festus and run out to the Sileys' place and see if you can get any more information on that stolen tractor. Interview the neighbors, drive the back roads, and check that abandoned barn two miles south of their place."

"We've done all that already, boss," he anxiously complained. Jordan didn't clue in on the motive for the order but turned to comply as the sheriff turned an angry eye upon him. "Yes sir. Do you want us to report back in an hour or so then?"

"Just get going, Jordan."

No sooner had Jordan and Festus left the building than CJ hit the door and stormed into Jeremiah's office. With that long blond hair flowing past her shoulders, in her powder-blue suit, standing there all defiant and angry, Jeremiah just wanted to pull her to him and give her the long, slow kiss that she needed. Instead, he turned and faced her, waiting for the worst of the storm to blow in.

***

CJ was so angry, she couldn't think. The heat outside and her march across the street brought a bead of sweat to her forehead, and she took a moment to collect her thoughts and wipe a drip away before it ran down her cheek. She looked up at Jeremiah. He was taller than her now and exuded a quiet strength that she had come to respect and admire. He looked handsome in his uniform, but what drew her most were his piercing blue eyes.

"I need a favor, Jeremiah," she said. It wasn't a question, and she braced for the compromise she was sure to have to offer in order to get it. When Jeremiah didn't say anything, she continued. "Winkey has ordered me to do a hundred and fifty hours of community service in the form of pro bono work. I need access to the district attorney's files so I can handpick the cases I'm assigned to before I accept the offer."

"I assume you're talking to me again then?" When she didn't answer, he went on. "What if I don't help you, CJ? What happens then?" he quietly asked as he took a seat on the edge of his desk.

Jeremiah was a man who liked details and without them, CJ knew he wouldn't help her. She had less than an hour to get the information she needed and get back to the judge's chambers with an answer before she faced jail time. The clock was ticking. Knowing she was caught between a rock and a hard place, CJ was reluctant to give details, but Jeremiah was a stubborn man. He talked slow, but that didn't mean he wasn't quick-witted, and she'd never once lied to him. She wasn't about to start now, but that didn't mean she had to give the whole story.

"I have a choice. I can spend thirty days in your jail or do the pro bono cases. I'm not walking into a workload that I'm stuck with for the next four months. You know that once I start something, I can't leave it alone until it's done. I just want an opportunity to put some boundaries on the cases I'm given before I accept, that's all."

Charlie Joe watched as Jeremiah looked down at his boots in a vain attempt to stifle a smile. Judge Winkler and Jeremiah's father had been good friends since the dawn of time. The judge was well apprised of Jeremiah's feelings towards her. Although Jeremiah didn't know the details of her current predicament, she knew he would guess the motive for this new development. The district attorney was an old college friend of Jeremiah's, and CJ understood if she asked, Jeremiah could make it happen for her.

"If I do this thing for you, what's in it for me?" he asked, looking down into her pretty green eyes.

CJ knew this was coming and was prepared for it. "My birthday is today, Jeremiah. Consider it a present to me."

"No deal," he said. She wasn't getting off that easily.

"Well then, what do you want?"

Jeremiah just sat there, smiling at her. She knew what he wanted, and he knew she wasn't ready to get married. He'd wait—forever if he had to. Charlie Joe stepped forward and grabbed him by his shirtfront.

"Jeremiah Stone," she whispered as she looked into his eyes. It was a weakness she knew about him, how she could whisper something and watch him melt to her commands. She was pulling out the big guns, but Jeremiah wasn't so easily swayed. He pulled back as he stood up and put his strong hands over hers. Firmly holding her hands in place, he tugged her closer before speaking.

"I'll do this thing you ask, CJ, but don't pull any punches with me." She watched his eyes as he spoke. She had worn perfume today and wondered if he'd lost his train of thought because of it. Small feminine wiles came in handy from time to time. She smiled thinking how she was driving him crazy just now.

"You do this for me, Jeremiah. I won't forget it, I promise. You have my word," she offered, leaving herself open for a potentially unfavorable negotiation position. That was fine. Jeremiah would never hurt her, so she could trust him. She just couldn't bring herself to walk down the aisle of doom yet. She knew what was holding her back. She had to know who her birth parents were. She wanted to meet them. Until she figured it out how to make that happen, she was holding her ground, even if it meant losing the man she knew she loved.

She pulled back as he relaxed his hold on her hands. She saw a flicker of sadness there, right before he dropped his hands, but she couldn't bring herself to think on it right now.

"Will you come with me over to the district attorney's office? Talk to him now?"

"What's the hurry, CJ?" he asked.

"If I'm not back in Winkey's courtroom in thirty minutes, I get the can," she admitted.

Jeremiah burst out laughing as he walked past her and opened the door for her. "Darling, I think I'd rather have the devil in my clink than a hellcat like you. But remember, this is two that you owe me now."

"What do you mean?" she asked defiantly.

"The Siley's missing tractor, CJ."

"Whatever do you mean, Sheriff Stone?"

"We both know what I mean," he said as she walked past him, and he pulled the door to his office closed. Her ears weren't red anymore, but she was blushing. Charlie Joe did in fact know something about that missing tractor, but she wasn't about to fess up to anything. Not yet.

8

Sweetwater, Missouri, December

Lance Meton sat with Meretrix in his car on the side of a road next to an unharvested corn crop. Rain had settled in and as the temperature dropped, ice began to form on his windshield. Since the gas gauge was near empty, he turned the car off and waited in the dark. Being broke and almost out of gas was just the tip of the iceberg for Lance. His last cocaine drop had not gone down favorably, and tonight's meeting was going to be unpleasant for him, he knew. The chill of the wind began to quickly creep through the car. He pulled the hood of his light jacket, the only coat he had, over his head and tucked his hands under his legs to help keep them warm, watching the road ahead of him for car lights. Meretrix sat silently next to the passenger door.

"He's twenty minutes late," she whispered as she shivered. Meretrix had met Lance at a party in Kansas City a year ago, introducing him to a dark and very dangerous underworld. His quick mind and patient temperament had impressed a dealer named Mombasa, and a bargain was made between the two. Lance would traffic drugs to Wichita, Kansas twice a month and make a significant profit with each successful drop. Up until last week, nothing had gone wrong.

"He's never late," she said, obviously worried.

"What do you want me to do about it?" he said. The woman was beautiful to look at, but a minx to deal with on a regular basis. The tension of the night was building inside him, and his bowels were rumbling. His intuition screamed "Leave! Leave!" But he knew that if he didn't keep this appointment tonight, matters would become much, much worse.

He looked over at Meretrix and wondered if she would break down and tell them what happened in Wichita. He loathed her for seeing him fail, and the knowledge she harbored could be used to her advantage.

"Car," she whispered as headlights appeared in the distance.

The white Lincoln Continental, covered in mud, slowed to a stop, and two men got out, walking into the beam of the headlights.

Meretrix glanced over at Lance. "Show time," she said as she opened her door and stepped out into what was now a growing ice storm. A chill ran down Lance's spine as he opened his door to join the three in the headlights between the two cars. As he did so, another smaller man emerged from the backseat of the Lincoln. *Mombasa* thought Lance.

Mombasa walked around his two men and stood in front of Lance and Meretrix. Looking at both of them as they stood, freezing in the rain, he pulled his long overcoat open and drew out a gun. Pointing it at Meretrix's forehead, he looked at Lance and executed her. Blood and bone splattered all over Lance, and he jumped at both the shock of what had just happened and the realization that he would be next.

***

Rachelle balanced the phone on her little shoulder as she watched her sister walk down the hallway to take the trash outside. Once Riley was out the door, Rachelle quietly dialed the number her parents had made her memorize for emergencies.

"Nine-one-one, what is your emergency?" the female dispatcher calmly asked.

"My sister won't cut my ba-sketti," Rachelle said.

"Where are you at right now?" the dispatcher questioned.

"At home," Rachelle said. "My sister made me ba-sketti and she won't cut it for me." Hearing the back door open and close again, Rachelle quickly ended the conversation and hung up the phone, racing back to the kitchen table before Riley could see what she had done.

It was noon on Saturday. Riley had made spaghetti for lunch, and she had just sat down at the piano when the phone rang.

"You're going to get it now!" Rachelle sing-songed from her place at the kitchen table. Spaghetti sauce colored the front of her white cotton sweater. She sat licking her fingers, smiling triumphantly as Shirley walked in the door.

"Mom!" Rachelle cheered.

"Mom, the police are on the phone. They want to talk to you," Rachelle said as she walked back toward the foyer and handed Shirley the phone.

"Yes?" she asked. Shirley quietly listened to the dispatcher retell the call she had received. "No, I'm sorry. Everything is fine here. I apologize. Thank you for calling." She hung up the phone. Turning to Riley she asked, "What happened while I was gone?"

Riley rolled her eyes and turned back to the Bach piece she wanted to work on before answering. "I made spaghetti, and Rachelle wanted me to cut it for her. I refused to do it. She's in school now. She can start doing some things for herself. I didn't know she called nine-one-one." Riley looked around her mom to glare at Rachelle in the kitchen.

"She was being mean to me!" Rachelle said.

Shirley said a silent prayer for patience as she shrugged out of her coat and hung it up in the closet. As she stepped out of her snow boots, she looked toward Rachelle.

"We need to have a chat about when to call nine-one-one and when to *not* call nine-one-one, Rachelle. Your sister refusing to cut your spaghetti is not an emergency. You know better than that."

Rachelle answered by pushing her plate away. Tears welled up in her eyes as she crossed her arms across her chest, her lower lip protruding. Shirley had seen this response numerous times, so she chose to ignore it for the time being. Rachelle had a sensitive temperament and coming down too hard on her often had poor results.

"When is your dad supposed to be home, Riley?" Shirley asked. "Do you know?"

"He didn't say when he'd be back. The pilot light on the furnace keeps blowing out, and Kevin had ball practice, so he ran to the hardware store after dropping Kevin off at the gym. Did you get a chance to call the music department at the college to see about classical piano teachers?"

Shirley didn't answer right away. Instead, she headed toward the thermostat. The house did feel a little cool, she thought. Although the ice storm had passed, the wind was still blowing pretty hard outside and keeping the temperatures hovering in the twenties. She kicked the thermostat up a few degrees and walked to the register on the floor. After a few minutes, the furnace kicked on and blew out cold air.

"How long has your dad been gone?" she asked. Shirley had always depended on Stuart to take care of these kinds of things. She didn't have a clue where to find the pilot light on the furnace, let alone how to light it.

"About thirty minutes or so," Riley said.

"I have my Christmas letter done for Santa, Mom! Can we mail it today?" Rachelle pleaded as she moved in front of her mom to get her full attention.

"Of course, Rachelle," she said as she bent to pick her up. Rachelle's bare feet were cold to her touch. Moving toward the bedroom, she called back to Riley, "Call your dad on his cell phone and ask him when he'll be home."

Riley got up from the piano bench and followed her mom down the hallway. "The sheriff's office has called twice. Dad must have forgotten to charge his phone again. They want him to call in right away when he gets home."

Shirley rifled through a pile of clean clothes on the bed, looking for a pair of socks for Rachelle. Laundry was a never-ending chore, and piling clean clothes on the bed in the spare room allowed them to keep up with the laundry while also being able to close the door on it when guests came over.

"Oh, and I'm going over to Janet's house for dinner tonight. We're going to work on her song for the 'Winter Program' next Friday," she scoffed, using air quotes. "I don't know why they don't just call it the Christmas Program. And what about a piano teacher?" Riley was eager to start moving forward with her music again. She had thought that either Julliard or Curtis would be good choices for her, but she'd never hope for scholarships if she didn't find a good teacher, and soon.

"They are just trying to be politically correct, Riley. It's the way of the world right now," Shirley said as she tugged Rachelle's socks onto her tiny feet, wondering if her daughter had grown, or if the socks had shrunk. Rachelle sat on the bed, her letter to Santa grasped firmly in her little hand.

"I e-mailed the music department, Riley, but haven't heard anything yet. I imagine that since they are going into finals soon, they won't get back to me right away. I'm going to put a roast in the oven to help keep the house warm this afternoon," she thought out loud as she walked back toward the kitchen. At least she had gotten some of her Christmas shopping done this morning. The house still needed to be decorated and the tree put up, but the kids could do that tomorrow after church. There's just so much to do during the holidays, she thought, and time seemed to fly by faster with each passing year.

"Mommy. I need this letter mailed today. It's important!" Rachelle said.

Shirley took the letter from Rachelle and noticed that she had drawn spades allover the envelope. "What are these drawings for, Rachelle?"

"They are from my dream. I'm asking Santa to pray to protect my big sister."

"What dream, Rachelle?"

"I had a dream that a big mean monster with these funny marks on his arms was coming to hurt my big sister. Jesus said she would be okay, but that I needed to pray for her."

"Riley is right here, Rachelle. It was just a dream. Would you like to write another letter to Santa?"

"I have another big sister, Mommy. You know that." Rachelle laid her head down on Shirley's shoulder, the letter still grasped in her hand. "It's important that I mail it today."

Shocked and unable to respond, Shirley hugged Rachelle tight. *How does she know? I have the decorative box hidden away, too high for Rachelle to ever reach on her own. The twins have never said anything, so they can't possibly know either. Stuart would never have said anything.* "Can Daddy and I read it before we mail it?"

"Okay, Mommy. You and Daddy can read it if you promise to mail it for me."

9

Blackhorse, Missouri

Charlie Joe had spent the better part of the day down in the district attorney's office working on the cases that she had been handling for the last couple of weeks. Although she was able to pick some of the cases assigned, the DA hadn't let her have full rein over her assignment and so she had been handed two additional cases above the four that she chose to accept. She had to be in court on Monday and needed to come down to Moses's shop to check on a private matter while she had the chance. Christmas was fast approaching, and time was closing in on her.

The shop was nothing more than a renovated old barn with a cement floor and a wood stove added for comfort. Moses, a tall, muscular black man who played running back for Mississippi State during his college years, earned a business degree before coming home to open a machine shop behind his parents' house. He did a brisk business from all four counties and was known for being honest and trustworthy, as well as being a damn good mechanic and welder. He had been expecting CJ to come around, and when he saw her, he had everything laid out, ready for her inspection.

"Hey, Moses!" Charlie Joe smiled as she came through the door, careful to close it securely before venturing farther into the shop. The sun had gone down, and the wind had a chilling bite to it tonight. She wore a dark-brown leather jacket with a thick wool scarf and mittens to keep the cold at bay. Her nose and cheeks glowed red, giving away the effects of the chilling air. The heater in her 1976 Dodge truck quit working again a few months back, and although Moses had offered to fix it for her, she declined, saying she couldn't do without a ride just now. She had court to attend to and other matters that required her to have reliable transportation. The truck was her daddy's, and as long as the engine ran, she was remiss to part with it, even for a short while.

She missed her parents this time of year. She hadn't been out to their graves in some time.

"CJ!" Moses greeted her, wiping his hands on a dirty rag as he came forward. The rusted-out Chevy truck stood with its hood up, parts methodically placed on the clean cement floor in a semicircle around his work area. A little red VW bug and a '08 Mustang sat in the bays on either side of the Chevy, waiting their turn with the engine surgeon to do his magic.

"Have you picked out your cummerbund yet?" she teased. Moses had been in love with Sarah Jane for almost two years now and had finally asked her to marry him. A January wedding was planned, and the thought of Moses in a tux, well, it just didn't fit his person very well. Overalls and work boots were more his style.

"Aww, you know women. I'll be trussed up like a thanksgiving turkey, but if that's what it takes, I'm willin' to do it for her," he said as he walked toward the back of his shop. "Your big project is done and ready for delivery, CJ." Commissioned pieces were not something Moses did on a regular basis, but he enjoyed the work, as it was a nice change from the everyday mechanical jobs he usually did. "Why you spending this money on Ol' Man Siley's tractor, CJ? Stealin' the tractor, getting it remodeled, what did you do that you're tryin' to make right?"

Charlie Joe took a deep breath before answering. Moses was a good friend. She knew she could trust him. "Remember when we were kids and the police found that tractor in the pond?"

"Oh my word, CJ! Was that the Siley's tractor?" Moses' whole body shook as he began laughing. "Your Momma would woop your butt if she knew you were the one who'd done that!"

"I'm *trying* to make it right aren't I? Besides, I wasn't the only one involved that day. Jeremiah was right there with me." CJ smiled as she remembered how Jeremiah clung to the fender of the tractor, screaming like a little girl all the way down the hill. She was too small to reach the breaks. Stopping just wasn't in the cards that day. Funny how Jeremiah never lets her drive when they go somewhere together now. "Stealth and secrecy are paramount to the success of this particular project, Moses. I know I don't have to remind you, but do you have anyone to help you with the delivery yet?" she asked, admiring the fine paint job on the machine in front of her.

"My cousin has a flatbed trailer and truck. His two boys will be there to help too. I'm not real worried about off-loading it, CJ. My real concern is the police. They've been up and down every county road this side of the Mississippi. If I get caught with this thing on Christmas Eve, it won't be pretty," he warned.

"I have a plan for that, Moses. You just worry about getting it delivered. I'll take care of the police, and Moses?" Charlie Joe paused to make sure he was looking at her before continuing. "Thank you for doing this for me. I've wanted to make this right for a long time and since Mr. Siley had his heart attack, I think it will be a perfect Christmas surprise for him."

"Yes ma'am. It's a right nice thing you're doing." Moses smiled. CJ was as good as her word, and he trusted her. Moses gave a quiet chuckle, thinking about how Miss Charlie Joe was going to go about taking care of the police, and it gave him a warm feeling to be part of this good deed of hers. "When do you want the big delivery to happen?"

"Ten days, Moses. One a.m. on Sunday will work just fine." She grinned.

"You know I'll do my very best."

10

Officer Hank Lawson was out of town for his sister's wedding, so Sheriff Langdon took the dispatch call when it came over the radio. He was sitting in the squad car doing traffic detail on an old section of Highway 65 when he got the frantic call from Doris Hall. She worked dispatch over at the station and had been a permanent fixture there for almost thirty years. If Doris was upset, it must be something big, he thought.

"An out-of-town hunter coming in from a tree stand found a body on a low-maintenance road just this side of the county line," Doris breathlessly yelled into the mic. "No other information is available at this time, boss." She gave the exact location of where the call had come from. The hunter was waiting for the police to arrive. Sheriff Langdon didn't need to write the location down, as he knew the area well. It was adjacent to his daddy's farm in the Lamine River bottom ground.

Rifle season had just ended, but archery season for the white-tailed deer was still open. This part of Missouri attracted a lot of hunters. Heavy timber coverage and broad stream valleys indigenous to the area provided copious amounts of coverage for the white-tailed deer, making them plentiful. As beautiful as they were to look at, they could be deadly to oncoming traffic. In recent years the number of fatal car accidents caused by deer on the highways had climbed and the Department of Wildlife had responded by increasing the number of deer tags issued this season. It didn't surprise him that an out-of-towner was tramping through his territory, looking for game this time of year.

Sheriff Langdon picked up his radio and dispatched back to town. "I need you to call in Detective Stuart Riedel," he ordered as he pulled out onto the highway. "If you can't reach him on the phone, send someone out to find him."

***

Stuart was frustrated. The hardware store was closed, and the roads were too bad to drive to the next town for the parts he needed to fix the furnace. His cell phone was dead, so he couldn't call Shirley and let her know what was going on. He sat in his truck, contemplating what to do next, when Doris Hall pulled up next to him.

He had met her right after starting his new job with the sheriff's office. Mrs. Hall was short and round, with an easy smile and a quick temper. He'd seen her go rounds with Hank Lawson a time or two over a call that came in that she felt he didn't respond to quick enough. On the whole, she was more competent than most dispatchers in the larger cities, and he felt he could trust her. Her anxious demeanor now worried him as he stepped out of his truck to meet her.

"I've been trying to reach you for over a hour, Detective Riedel!" she scolded.

"I'm sorry, Doris, my phone is dead, and I didn't realize it until just now," he said.

"A hunter found a dead body out near the Browning place. Do you know where that is?" When he didn't immediately answer, she turned back to her car. "Get in," she ordered. "I'll take you out there."

"Doris, my equipment is in my car at home. I'll have to go back there first and get it, then I can follow you out. Oh, and hey, my furnace went out at home. Is there someone you can call to go out and either replace it or fix it for me? Obviously, I won't be able to take care of that today, and in this weather, I can't just let it go."

Doris was a paradigm of efficiency. Before they reached his house on Oliver Drive, she had called her sister's cousin's brother-in-law and made arrangements for a new furnace to be put in that very afternoon. Stuart wasn't sure if he should be ecstatic that it was done and his home would be warm again, or worried. He decided he'd just take care of police business and let everything else fall into place as he changed cars and let Shirley know he wouldn't be home anytime soon.

***

Mombasa hadn't said a word before getting back into his Lincoln and driving away, but the message had been clear. It had been two days, and Lance still shook when he thought about the execution of Meretrix. They had sex together, and did cocaine drops together, but outside those activities, they were strangers, and over time found that they didn't particularly like each other. Witnessing her murder had superficially created feelings for Meretrix that hadn't been there before, and he wondered if it was born of fear or sympathy.

He went into the bathroom of the two-bedroom bungalow he and his mother shared on the edge of town. It was an old house, and the wind crept through cracks in the wall and under the doors. He bought some plastic to seal the windows for the winter for his mom, and that had helped some, but it was still cold in the house, and a thin film of ice rested in the toilet bowl. He closed the door and let the water in the freestanding sink run until it was warm, then splashed his face. His mom worked nights at the factory in Hamilton and slept days. His dad was in prison, but he didn't think that was common knowledge around town. Lance was on his own, in more ways than one, he thought.

Looking up into the mirror above the sink, Lance took stock of himself. The drug money was gone, taken in Wichita. Meretrix was dead. Mombasa expected all drops to go perfectly. Meretrix had mentioned in the beginning that the drug lord had eyes at every drop and knew minute details about each soul who worked for him. Lance didn't doubt that if he tried to back out or quit doing drops, someone would die, and it would most likely be him. He was in deep. He was afraid, and he didn't know what to do. The one good thing in his life was Riley Riedel. Just thinking about her made him smile, but the dark cloud of fear hovered in his mind. What he needed was a way out, and to that end, he began to formulate a plan.

11

Blackhorse, Missouri

Audrey Lemoine had recovered from her courtroom attack and was back at her job as a teller in the State Bank. The kids had two more weeks of school before they were off on break, and she was thinking about sending them to her mother's house for a few days for a nice holiday visit when June and Carl Siley walked into the bank foyer. From the looks of June's swollen eyes, Audrey could tell she'd been crying and came around the counter to meet them.

"Well, hello!" she cheerily greeted them. "It's so good to see you two again. What can I do for you today?" she asked.

"We need to see that bank manager," Carl said.

"Is there something wrong, Carl?" Audrey gently asked.

"Audrey, you know that Carl was in the hospital for his heart two months back," June said. "The medication he has to take isn't covered by his insurance." Audrey could see the pain in their faces as June continued. "Our old Ford tractor was needing some work on the engine before it was stolen, and we're afraid that since the hospitalization and the mounting bills, we are going to be a few months late on payments. We are just sick about it being stolen. We can't afford to replace it. The police haven't found it yet, and the way things are looking, we won't ever see it again."

"Now don't give up hope, June," Audrey said. "At the very least, your insurance company will cover the loss, but I have a feeling it won't come to that." She paused before she continued. "I recently started handling all the loan accounts in addition to working the drive-through teller position. I don't recall seeing any late payments on your account. Come on over to my desk and let me check on the computer." Audrey lured them over to her small brown desk at the side of the foyer. The couple sat in the two chairs in front of her desk and anxiously watched as Audrey opened their loan accounts and brought up the one in question.

"Here it is," she said as she turned the monitor around for them to see. "Your account for the tractor is paid up through May of next year. It looks like you made a large payment on that piece of equipment just last month."

"That can't be right," Carl said. "I wasn't able to harvest my corn crop this year as I was laid up in the hospital. Insurance money is pending and I certainly don't have that kind of cash just lying around to make a large payment like that. Your records must be wrong."

"I'll get the bank manager and have him look at it for us. Can you wait here a minute, please?" Audrey stood and made her way to the manager's office.

Justin Malone had transferred into the bank as a new manager just last year and was still getting to know his clients. He remembered the Sileys, as they were so friendly and forthright. He and Audrey spoke briefly in the privacy of his office before he walked back over to where they were sitting.

"Mr. and Mrs. Siley!" he said as he offered them both a friendly handshake. "What a pleasure to see you today. Audrey says that you have some questions regarding one of your loan accounts."

"She tells us it has been paid up through May of next year, Mr. Malone," Carl said. "I didn't make a payment on that account last month. That's why we are here today. We can't make payments on it right now."

Justin looked over at the monitor and reviewed the account information as Carl finished speaking. "Well, Mr. Siley, we balance our books every night here, so I know that the deposit made last month is accurate, but I can have Audrey review the books again to make sure. However, I remember the day this payment came through. One of the tellers brought it to me, as it came to the bank in the form of a wire transfer to your account. I'm the only one in the building with authorization to accept wire transfers over five thousand dollars, and I handled this payment myself. Company policy, you see."

The Sileys were shell-shocked. "Who sent the payment?" Carl asked.

Justin Malone looked back at the screen and clicked into the account history to see if access to this information was available.

"All I show is the routing number from the account it was transferred from. No other information is available, I'm afraid, Mr. Siley; but I assure you, the transfer was legitimate, and you are paid in full through next May. Oh, wait. There's a note here on the wire transfer. It says that there is a card for you here in the bank." Justin Malone looked up at Audrey. "Do you know anything about a card?"

"Yes, as a matter of fact, I do. It came in the in the mail last week. I was going to forward it, but forgot until now." Audrey walked back to her desk and retrieved a large red envelope from the drawer on the side of her desk. She walked back to Mr. Siley and handed it to him.

He opened the card and as he read the message, tears welled up in his eyes.

"What's it say, Mr. Siley?"

"It just says, '*Thanks for all the lovely watermelons we ate growing up. They were the best in the county. Sorry we stole them. Hope this makes up for it.*'"

12

Sweetwater, Missouri

Riley stepped out onto the stage in a long, sequined, black dress and sat at the Steinway piano that was placed in the middle of the stage. With her long hair swept up with a comb, she looked every inch the professional as she rested her hands on her thighs to compose herself. Mozart Concerto no. 24 in C Minor was her opening piece for the winter program. The piece was a favorite of hers, and she had been working on it for over a year, preparing it for competitions in the spring. She played for the full twelve minutes with tremendous emotion and flawless technique. The ebb and flow of the melody reverberated off the auditorium walls like the tides of an ocean, entrancing the audience with each new passage. A standing ovation rewarded her last chord, and she graciously stood, taking a bow before relinquishing the stage to the next performer. Kevin waited for her backstage. He gave her a big hug as she stepped behind the black curtains. She could always count on him to support her.

She gave a big sigh as she turned to watch the choir file in and mount the risers. Kevin leaned in to her and whispered, "Fantastic job, sis!"

She mouthed "Thank you" in return. He was a great brother, despite the many idiosyncrasies that drove her nuts. Janet came up beside them and grabbed Riley's hand. Janet was about to perform a solo piece with the choir standing behind her, and she needed the encouraging squeeze of a friend's hand before heading out to meet the lions. Riley put her arm around Janet's shoulder and gave her a squeeze before nudging her out past the side curtain.

The winter program lasted almost two hours before the final curtain closed to a round of catcalls and applause. The kids involved had planned a post-performance party at Janet's house and were gathering their things and making ride arrangements when Lance came up behind Riley.

"Congratulations, Riley," he said. She looked stunning to him, and he couldn't take his eyes off her as she turned to acknowledge him.

"Thank you, Lance. I didn't know you were in the audience tonight," she said as she smiled at him. Lance was dressed in black dress pants, a black button-down shirt and a pale-blue tie. He'd gotten his hair cut too, Riley noticed.

"Are you kidding? I wouldn't miss it for all the money in Missouri," he admitted. His heart was beating hard in his chest as he made his next move. "Can I give you a ride home?"

"I'm going to Janet's house for a post-performance party, Lance. Kevin has the car tonight, as he has to turn in early for a game tomorrow, and I was going to hitch a ride with Amy and Dylan."

"I can drop you off if you like," he responded, hoping she'd accept.

Riley thought for a moment as she looked around the room. She didn't see Amy or Dylan anywhere and decided it would be all right for her to accept Lance's offer. After all, it was just a few blocks from the school.

"Let me change my clothes first, Lance, then we can go," she said. "I don't want anything to happen to this dress." She turned to walk toward the lady's room at the end of the hall.

"I'll meet you in the foyer then, Riley." Lance smiled. His heart leaped in his chest, and his cheeks flushed with the excitement of having her accept a ride from him.

Riley emerged from the lady's room in faded low-rise jeans and a cardigan sweater. Her hair was still swept up in the comb, and with the amount of hair spray she had applied, she was afraid to take the comb out for fear of the mess her hair would become. She found Lance waiting in the foyer. Most of the parents had already left the school, including her parents, but a few milled about visiting with the teachers who remained. Lance offered to take her gym bag and dress as she slipped into her red wool pea coat. Once she was buttoned up against the cold, they headed out the school doors toward the parking lot.

They passed Officer Hank Lawson on the sidewalk outside. He had come to the performance with Miss Henry, the new music and drama instructor, and he was waiting for her to finish up inside before they left.

"Hey there, Lance, Riley." He acknowledged them both as they approached. "Where are you two off to tonight?"

"Hello, Officer Lawson," Riley responded. "Just headed over to the Nelsons for a post-performance party." Riley sensed some tension from Lance as they passed but didn't mention anything to him about it as she put her hand on his arm.

"You keep out of trouble now, you hear?" Officer Lawson said.

Riley turned back to face him as she walked away. "I'm not sure that you aren't the one we should be worried about, sir!" she teased, trying to lighten a moment of tension. Lance laughed at Riley's retort and smiled down at her. It was a beautiful moment for him, having her take his arm and hear her laughter in his presence.

Neither Riley nor Lance had any idea how true to the mark her retort was, thought Officer Lawson as he watched them cross the parking lot and get into Lance's car.

They arrived at the Nelsons' home a few minutes later. Lance got out and came around to Riley's side of the car to open her door for her. She stepped out and stood between the door and Lance for a moment.

"Lance, why don't you come in with me?" she said. He had been nice to her for weeks, always smiling and saying hello and never asking anything of her. Kevin had mentioned that she should steer clear of him, but he couldn't tell her why she should listen to his advice. What she had witnessed of his character was that he was a country boy castoff. In other words, he didn't fit into the small-town community. He was smaller in size than most of the farm kids who went to their school, but he was smart and always respectful. She noticed that he refused to say the Pledge of Allegiance, but he always stood in respect to others when they recited the Pledge. His open independence didn't make him a criminal and certainly didn't mean there was anything wrong with him. He was quiet and stayed to himself most of the time. He had a few tattoos that the teachers were openly hostile about, but again, having tattoos didn't mean anything to her. She did notice that his attire had changed. When she first met him, he wore only black. Recently, though, he had started to wear more colors. His hair cut looked nice, too.

"I don't think your friends would like me to join you at the party, Riley. Maybe some other time." *The fact that she offered was proof enough that things were progressing as planned,* he thought. A very good sign indeed.

Riley looked toward the house for a moment, thinking. "You know, Lance, if you don't come in with me, I probably won't have a ride home," she challenged, looking back to him. She didn't know his history, but kindness was a good step in helping someone, and he had certainly showed her a kindness in offering her his friendship. She wanted to reciprocate and felt this was a good move.

Lance laughed at her audacity. "OK then. As a gentleman, I certainly can't refuse a lady in need. I'll come in for a little while with you." She was certainly full of surprises, he thought. Nothing like any girl he had ever met before. He had to be careful to watch his p's and q's while with her so as to not scare her off. *She is a class or two above me,* he thought, and to keep her interest, he would have to work hard.

She led the way up the walk to the front door and went in without ringing the doorbell. This surprised Lance some, as he had never had the kind of relationship with anyone where he felt free to enter that person's home unannounced. He followed her with some trepidation, not sure what kind of welcome he would receive.

***

Stuart had slipped into the winter program performance just as Riley sat down at the piano. He stood in the back of the auditorium until she had finished her piece, then found Shirley and Rachelle sitting in the middle section toward the front. An aisle seat had been saved for him, and he quietly moved down as the audience stood to give Riley the standing ovation she deserved. He was very proud of his daughter, he thought as he took his seat and prepared to watch the rest of the program. It was difficult for him, though, as the murder scene, thirteen days previous to tonight, was still very fresh in his mind.

The young woman had been executed at point-blank range, suggesting that the killer knew her well enough to be close to her. Sheriff Will Langdon didn't recognize her as being from the local area, which suggested that she was either driven to the spot of execution or someone met her there. Two sets of tire tracks, each from separate directions, gave Stuart a feeling of a meeting gone bad.

His thoughts were broken as Janet Nelson walked out onto the stage with the choir at her back. Standing with a confidence uncommon for her, she took the microphone, smiled into the lights, and began the "Queen of the Night" aria from Mozart's *The Magic Flute*. The strength of her voice reverberated to the back of the auditorium.

Shirley and Stuart looked at each other in amazement. Riley had been going over to Janet's house for weeks, helping her prepare for this performance, but they had never heard her sing. The audience was silent, and as she hit her last note, Stuart felt his eyes tear up a little. Again, the audience stood to honor another of their own with a robust ovation. The unexpected strength and confidence of her voice would be talked about for weeks, and he knew her parents were very proud of her at this moment.

Janet took her bow and left the choir on stage to begin their winter selections for the duration of the program. As the crowd settled back, his thoughts unexpectedly turned to the little girl he and Shirley had given up for adoption. He took a hanky from his back pocket to dry his eyes. This sudden well of emotion took him off guard. He occasionally thought of her and wondered what had become of her, but he felt an uncommon urge to pray at that moment. He didn't know why, or what for, but it was there, and he couldn't ignore it.

Lord, I can sense that I should pray for our little girl. I don't know where she is or what she's up to, but I just want you to remember her. Maybe she somehow has a need to know us or meet us; I don't know, but I ask that you be with her, protect her, and help her find whatever it is that she needs. In Christ's name I pray. Amen.

"Are you OK, Stuart?" Shirley quietly asked, concern written all over her face as she sought to make eye contact with him.

"Yes, I'm fine," he lied, being careful to not look at her as he spoke.

"The case is bothering you, isn't it?" she whispered as she leaned toward him. Rachelle had climbed up on her lap and was snuggling down into her shoulder as if to fall asleep. Shirley knew that Stuart personally owned every case he worked, and because of it, each case weighed heavily upon him until he could solve it. It was a bad habit of his, because not every case had a neat and tidy ending. In fact, many did not. She shifted Rachelle to a more comfortable position as the choir began again. The location of their lives had certainly changed with the move, but the concerns and worries followed them still.

Stuart didn't respond to Shirley. She knew him well enough to know that the murder investigation would eat at him until he could find the killer. It struck him that maybe this one hit closer to home for him because the victim was about the same age as their first child would be right now. *Maybe that's why I keep feeling like I should pray for her,* he thought. Shirley had shown him Rachelle's letter to Santa. It had to be coincidence, or a child's fancy that Rachelle believed she had an older sister other than Riley. No one had ever spoken of the adoption. Shirley had her box of memories and letters she had written over the years, but they were well hidden and the children had never seen them. The spade shapes on the outside of Rachelle's letter shook him some. He hadn't told Shirley that Mombossa and Spade had made parole a few months back. How Rachelle had come to that particular design, with the particular idea of another older sister was beyond him. Rachelle had said that she had had a dream; that the older sister was in danger, but that Jesus would protect her if she prayed.

It was all just hitting close to home, and that had never really happened to him before. *It could also be because of being shot*, he reasoned, trying to pin down exactly why he was having a hard time with this particular case. He had an odd sense that there was more to it, though, and that sense stayed with him. *Mombasa and Spade couldn't possibly know I'm here. They can't be linked to this murder, this town, or anyone in it. It can't be them*, he reasoned.

The particulars of the murder ran through his mind as the program continued. Execution with a .38 caliber handgun. The bullet casing, found in the mud just a few feet from the body, had specific and uncommon rotation markings on it, suggesting the gun that was used had been specially made or altered for the shooter. Two sets of tire tracks. Five sets of footprints. The body in the morgue over at county hospital had been identified as Mary Ellen O'Connor. Age twenty-eight. Height five-foot nine. Weight one hundred and fifty-four pounds. Her origins had been traced back to Olathe, a suburb just south of Kansas City. Unmarried. No children. No siblings. Her parents had been located and interviewed. She had started running with a rough crowd about ten years ago. Although she didn't do drugs that they knew of, she did turn a trick or two as a police rap sheet confirmed. She had no identification and no money on her person at the time of discovery.

Forensics was still working its magic for minute detailed evidence on the body, but that was the extent of his gross evidence to this point. With the encouragement of Sheriff Will Langdon, but against Stuart's better judgment, he held off on interviewing anyone younger than eighteen about any knowledge or association with the victim, but he did interview a number of townsfolk. No real leads at this point, but that didn't mean they weren't there. He just needed to continue bulldogging the case and working the streets. Being new in town made him feel like a rookie again, and having Officer Hank Lawson hawk-eyeing him at every corner was putting him on edge. Stuart knew he was just being sensitive, but it still bothered him, this constant vigilance of Officer Lawson. *Maybe what I ought to do is give my buddy Matthew Johnson back at the US marshal's office a call,* Stuart thought. *Just touch base with him.*

***

Moving to a new school in junior year was tough enough, but coming into it as an athlete who was used to being captain of the team made the transition a little dicier for Kevin. His natural leadership ability had prevented a few blows already, but pride tended to block the way to forging quick friendships. Kevin felt more like a gladiator on the team, with the constant testing of wills and pecking order still taking place. Dylan Forrester, the young man he had made friends with at the Nelsons' barbecue before school started, seemed to be the only person he could consistently trust and look to for support and encouragement. Dylan had also been his biggest rival for team captain, which made losing that position a little less painful for him.

The team had managed to squeak past the Wellsville Warriors the night before with a 56–54 win on the books. As Kevin lay in his bed the morning after the game, he recalled the highlights of the game and the ride home.

What really stuck in his mind was the discussion of the murder out by the Browning Place two weeks ago. The police had not yet interviewed the youth in the area, and the kids were speculating as to why. They had seen the girl around at parties on the weekends. Some of them had even talked to her the weekend her body was found, and it scared them. The boys on the team knew Kevin's dad was investigating the case and point-blank asked him why the school kids weren't being interviewed. Kevin wasn't in the habit of talking to his dad about his cases. In fact, his dad rarely discussed work at home. Afraid that some little piece of information vital to a case would somehow slip into the wrong hands, his dad diligently guarded case data from all but those who were directly involved. This was a different matter in Kevin's mind, though. His teammates had wanted information, and he couldn't accommodate that request, but he could certainly talk to his dad and find out why the investigation didn't involve the kids who knew her.

Kevin swung his legs over the side of the bed and shuffled down the hall to the bathroom. He could hear Rachelle talking to Mom in the kitchen and knew that Riley would be out jogging about this time of day. He thought she was nuts to jog in this cold weather. Staying under nice warm covers was much more appealing to him than torturing yourself with freezing air and pounding pavement.

He turned the shower on and stepped under the hot stream of water, letting it run down his back muscles and relax him. He had a term paper to finish today and a science test to study for before the day was through. Dylan wanted to go to Kansas City this afternoon to do some Christmas shopping and was swinging by to pick him up at two o'clock. He'd have to hustle to get everything done before then, he thought as he turned the water off and stepped out to towel off.

Wiping the steam off the mirror, he checked to see if he needed to shave. An even whisker growth splashed his face and made him look a bit rough. Kevin was a clean-cut kind of kid, so he got his electric razor out and did a quick job of it before heading back to this room to dress.

When he arrived at the kitchen, his mom had his favorite treat set out fresh for him. The smell of chocolate chip muffins had floated up to his room, making him hungry. He grabbed four off the plate and poured a glass of milk before turning to his mom.

"Where's Dad at today?" he asked.

Rachelle sat at the table drawing a picture with crayons while Shirley stood at the sink finishing up the dishes that wouldn't fit in the dishwasher. The warmth of the kitchen in direct contrast with the cold of the morning caused the windows to frost over, giving the room a "tucked in" feel.

"He couldn't find the paper on the drive this morning, so he headed down to Quik Mart to get one. He should be back any minute. What's on your agenda for the day?"

"I have a test to study for and a paper to finish. I'm riding with Dylan to KC this afternoon to do some Christmas shopping. Should be home around six o'clock tonight."

The front door opened, and a blast of cold air filled the kitchen. Stuart quickly closed and locked the door, stomping his feet to warm them as he shrugged out of his coat.

"Brrrrrr!" He shivered as he entered the kitchen with the paper in his hand. He pulled out a chair and sat down as Shirley brought a mug of hot coffee to the table for him. Stuart had already eaten breakfast.

"Morning, Kevin!" he said. "Great game you played last night."

Kevin looked up to him and smiled, his mouth full of muffin. He swallowed the last bite of muffin and took a long pull on his milk before speaking.

"Dad, I need to talk to you sometime today," he said, looking into his empty glass. "When would be a good time for you?"

Kevin didn't normally ask for an audience, so Stuart knew it must be important. "How about now?" Kevin rose from the table with his coffee mug and started toward the study he used for an office toward the back of the house. Stuart followed him into the room and closed the door.

Books lined the shelves along the north wall of the study. The heavy walnut desk, a family heirloom from Shirley's grandmother, sat in the middle of the room, with two wingback leather chairs arranged in front of it. Stuart sat in one of them as Kevin made his way to the picture window behind the desk. Looking out, he began.

"The kids at school are talking about the murder," he said. When Stuart didn't react, he continued. "Some of them knew the girl, but she was known by Meretrix instead of what the newspaper reported. They want to know why you aren't questioning them about what they know."

Stuart was used to Kevin's directness. It was a quality he admired in his only son. Honesty was the only reply he would offer, so he took a moment to form his answer so as to not mislead.

"We're new to this area, Kevin. We've only been here a few months. You understand as well as I do that working on a team is sometimes difficult, especially when you know that if things were handled differently, you would have less struggles with more successes. You and Dylan have been at odds with the basketball team and the plays that you run. In a way I'm running into the same issues on my team, the police department. Although you don't agree with what's going on on the team, you still respect your captain, do you not?"

Kevin could see where this conversation was headed. His dad had a way of saying things without really saying them. "Not to put too fine a point on it, Dad, what you are telling me is that you've been instructed to not question the kids who might have information about the case?"

"What I'm saying is this: boundaries have been set for me, and I don't fully understand the implications surrounding that decision. It certainly isn't helping the case, but he's my superior, and I have to respect those orders. However, I can't disqualify any information that might come my way by other means," he said with a knowing smile.

Understanding crossed Kevin's countenance, and he nodded his head in approval as he gazed back out the window into the huge yard with a mature oak tree standing sentry in the middle of it. It was a beautiful tree, Kevin thought. Bare of leaves this time of year, it still stood tall and strong against the angry winter winds that blew.

13

Jeremiah had just stopped by to drop a copy of the daily newspaper by Charlie Joe's house. The front-page story was about a young woman who had been shot execution style outside of Sweetwater, twenty miles away. Sheriff Will Langdon was a good friend of Jeremiah's and they called on each other's police force for occasional back up for parades, festivals, and such. A murder had not happened in this area for over fifty years. Suicides, yes. Murder, no. This was big news and he wanted to talk with her about it.

"What do you make of it, Jeremiah?" Charlie Joe took a sip of her coffee as she examined the paper at the kitchen table.

"I'm not sure. I called Sheriff Will and he said their new detective was working the case. His name is Stuart Riedel. He worked as a US Marshal until he was injured on the job. Moved to Sweetwater a few months ago. Will says he's Ace's; that he's really good at what he does. They think it was a professional hit."

Cranberry and white chocolate chip scones were baking in the gas stove and the aroma filled the kitchen while they spoke. Charlie Joe had not expected Jeremiah to be there that day, but now she was glad that she had gone ahead and baked them this morning. They were his favorite. The timer went off and she got up to take the scones out. As she moved towards the stove, the paper fell open on the floor. Jeremiah reached down to pick it up and noticed the story on the inside page.

"Here. Look at this, CJ. It's a special interest column on the new detective I was just telling you about." He folded the paper open to show the column and several photos of Detective Riedel, and his family.

Charlie Joe set the perfectly browned scones on top of the stove to cool before walking back to the kitchen table. "Nice family. The kids are really good looking; especially the little one. She's adorable."

The talk about family settled like stagnant water between them. Jeremiah let out a sigh and abruptly stood.

"I'd best be going, CJ. I'll leave the paper for you."

"Don't you want a scone before you go? They're your favorite!"

"Maybe some other time."

Jeremiah grabbed his hat from the little table standing by the front door. He didn't look back before he opened the door and hustled down the front porch steps and out to his truck. She could hear him start his engine and drive down her tree-lined driveway. December was a cold month of the year, but it had nothing on the chill Jeremiah had just left in the kitchen.

Something was wrong with Charlie Joe. She didn't know what it was, and she didn't know why she felt this way as she watched Jeremiah step off her front porch and get into his truck. She loved him. She truly did. Something inside her just held her back, kept her from accepting his hand in marriage. Of all the men she had ever known, he was the one who had captured her heart. She'd known since she was a little girl that she would marry him. She had told him as much more than once, but she thought she could see it in his eyes. He was giving up hope that dream would ever happen. She didn't like to see that in him. He was a good man. *Lord, what's wrong with me?* she prayed as she watched his truck drive down the driveway lined with oak trees.

It was a beautiful home with five bedrooms and a kitchen big enough to feed an army. It was built during the Civil War, and her daddy had spent the better part of his life keeping it up and making sure it was always in pristine condition. He was proud of the fact that his ancestors had worked as slaves in the cotton fields of this very place, and he had bought it with hard-earned money for his lovely bride.

She knew the story of her adoption. How her adoptive parents had tried for years to fill the house with children. How they felt the sting of barrenness. How God had brought Charlie Joe, a little white girl, into the home of a godly black couple with the laughter and joy that only a child can give. They had defied prejudice. Looked it full in the face and struggled to bring a divided community into the twenty-first century with their love and devotion for a little girl, *cast off by white parents who didn't have the love to give to their own kind.* The words burned into her thoughts. She wasn't sure she believed her biological parents didn't love her, but that thought still haunted her. She wanted to face them someday. She wanted to know why they had given her up for adoption. Did they not love her? How could someone cast off their own child? She needed answers to her past before she could face her future and the possibility of having children of her own.

Charlie Joe's momma had always told her that her biological parents gave her up because they loved her—that God had a plan—but Charlie Joe wasn't sure she believed it. She loved her adoptive parents, and wanted to believe the story her momma told, *but there it is*, she thought.

She had to do something, or she was going to lose Jeremiah. *Lord, please show me what to do,* she pleaded as she turned away from the window. *I don't understand this feeling inside. I love Jeremiah, and I don't want to lose him, but I can't bring myself to marry him. I've searched privately for years, even hired a private investigator, but have never been able to find out who my biological parents were. Are they still alive? What are they like? Are they still together? What happened that they gave me away?* Charlie Joe had so much love inside of her that she couldn't imagine being able to give up her own child. She just couldn't understand the why of it. She needed answers, and she needed them from the people who gave her up. She was beginning to fear that she would never meet them. What then? Could she let it go?

The ringing of the telephone startled her. She wiped the tears from her cheeks as she picked up the receiver of the old rotary dial telephone and answered as cheerily as she could for the moment. Cora Mae Vaxter was on the other end. Audrey was in trouble. Neil was at the house, drunk and trying to take the kids again.

"He has a gun, Charlie Joe."

"I'm on my way," she promised, wishing Jeremiah was still there with her. As she pulled on her jacket and headed for the door, a thought popped into her head. *Always saving others, aren't you, Charlie Joe? Who's gonna save you?*

14

Sweetwater, Missouri

It was four in the morning, and Lance had been driving since before midnight. He was exhausted, and the worst of the day hadn't even happened yet. Thankfully, school was out for the holiday break, so he didn't have to rush back to make it in time for class. The interstate roads had been pretty clear driving into Wichita, but the side streets were still a real mess to try to navigate. He'd made enough trips to the area that he pretty much knew what streets to take to avoid police detail. Carrying forty pounds of high-concentrate cocaine with a street value of $1,200,000 in his duffel bag in the backseat made him drive with excessive caution and alertness.

Pulling into the parking lot of the abandoned factory on the southwest side of town, he drove around the dark building and parked, turning his headlights off. He stayed in the car and waited for the white Hummer to arrive. He had never met the man he was to rendezvous with this morning. All he knew was that his new contact would be driving the white Hummer and identify himself as Spade. His old contact, he was told, was no longer "employed," meaning he was dead. Just thinking about it made Lance's stomach roll, but he girded his mind with other thoughts: thoughts of Riley.

Janet Nelson had taken a picture of them at the post-performance party that night, and Riley had given him a copy of it. He carried it in his wallet, and already the edges of the photo were frayed from him taking it out and looking at it so much. The interior of his car was too dark right now, and turning on the overhead light to look at it might draw unwanted attention. Besides, he had every line of her face memorized. He didn't need to see the picture to visualize her in his mind.

He relaxed in his seat as her memory flooded him. She had introduced him to her friends, and although they were cool in their greeting, most of them extended their friendship, including him in their jokes and conversations throughout the evening. Lance had even given James, a friend of Riley's, a ride home before seeing Riley to her door. He hadn't seen Riley outside school since that night, but he planned to change that very soon. He wouldn't go the whole break without seeing her again.

Headlights floated across the pavement at the far end of the lot. A security patrol car was making one last round before dawn. Lance hadn't expected this, and his mind raced with possible options as the headlights exposed his location and drew the attention of the guard. As the security vehicle approached, Lance glimpsed the white Hummer at the corner of the building behind and to the left of the approaching guard.

Keep your cool, Lance thought as he pushed back thoughts of Mombasa and what would surely happen if this drop blew.

The security guard stopped, keeping the head lamps on to reveal the passenger inside. He stepped out of the car, placing one hand on the gun in his holster, and approached Lance. A flashlight in the other hand, he knocked on the window and motioned for him to roll it down.

"Step out of the vehicle, please," he commanded.

Lance did as instructed, pulling his thin jacket closed to help keep the winter chill at bay as much as possible. The interior of his car had cooled some since he arrived, but standing in the cold December air blew all warmth away from his bones, and he gave an involuntary shutter.

"I need to see your driver's license and registration," the guard said.

Lance pulled his license and registration from his wallet and handed it to the guard. "Cold morning, Officer," he observed, venturing a stab at friendliness.

The officer did not reply, but handed back his license as he continued his interrogation. "What are you doing here at this time of day?"

"I'm meeting a friend," he half lied.

"What's in the bag?" he questioned, pointing out the gym bag in the backseat of the car.

Lance looked down at his shoes, giving himself a moment to collect his thoughts before answering. "I'm not a good basketball player, sir, and I really want to go to college. My friend is meeting me here tonight so we can drive out to Fort Hayes Community College. They are scrimmaging this afternoon, and I was hoping I could try walking on, maybe get a shot at a scholarship. My folks don't know I'm here, sir. I'd rather they don't find out about it, in case I don't make it."

The officer looked at Lance a moment, sizing him up, deciding if he was telling the truth or not. He was a tall kid and looked to be about the age of someone preparing for college. Remembering his own challenges at that age, he cut the kid some slack.

"This isn't the best part of town to be parking your car, son," he said. "When your friend gets here, I suggest you park somewhere else; otherwise, you may not have wheels when you get back."

"Thank you, Officer," he breathed. "I'll do that. Sure appreciate your concern."

"Good luck today," he said as he turned back to his security car.

Lance stood beside his car, giving a quick wave to the officer as he turned the car back around and drove off. He saw the front edge of the Hummer in the distance. Waiting.

Inside the Hummer, the barrel of a Blaser, Pro Camo Signal, 7mm Remington Mag had been sighted on the head of the security officer as he stood talking to Lance. A moment longer, and the Spade would have pulled the trigger. Watching the officer get back into the vehicle, he wondered what the kid had said to avoid suspicion and divert a certain disaster. He was beginning to understand why Mombasa favored this kid.

***

"Riley!" Shirley was tired of answering the phone all the time. Riley's friends were always calling, and she was seriously thinking that a cell phone would be a great Christmas present for her. She would have to talk to Stuart about it when he got home tonight.

"Riley! Phone!" she impatiently yelled up the stairs again.

"Coming!" Riley sing-songed as she raced down the hall to the upstairs phone. Janet was on the other end. Dylan and Amy were planning a hayrack ride and caroling event for the next night. Dylan was bringing his dad's John Deere 4020 tractor to town, with a flatbed trailer and some straw. Everyone was meeting at Janet's house at seven o'clock. They would take the hayride around town, stopping at several homes on the way to jump off and sing Christmas carols.

"Sounds like a blast, Janet!" Riley was ecstatic. She'd never been on a hayride before.

"Tell Kevin to come too, and Lance, if you want to invite him," Janet said. Lance had seemed nice at the last party she had, but there was something about him that made her feel uneasy. She tried to shake it off, and for the sake of her friendship with Riley, would try to make him feel welcome.

The girls planned to make hot cocoa and treats to bring on the ride, keeping people warm and in good cheer, as the temperature was predicted to drop into the low teens during the night. Part of the fun of doing it was suffering in the cold together and sharing warmth under the blankets, Janet confessed.

"I have some other news to share with you, Riley, but can't say anything over the phone," Janet said. "Why don't you come over this afternoon, and we can bake cookies and talk?"

"I can't today, Janet. I promised Rachelle we would put up the Christmas tree together and make cutout cookies. Mom is going Christmas shopping and will be gone all afternoon. Why don't you come over and join us?"

Janet arrived at the house at two o'clock, parking her little silver VW bug on the street and racing up the walk to the front door. Rachelle had been sitting in the window well watching for Janet and met her at the door before she had a chance to ring the bell.

"Hi, Rachelle," Janet greeted her as she came in and closed the door against the wind. Riley was already in the kitchen making the dough for the cutout cookies. Janet stood in the doorway to the kitchen as she peeled off her outer layers.

"Your house is so beautiful, Riley. I just love coming over here. It always looks like some magazine layout."

Riley laughed. "Mom is a real neat freak, so yes, the house stays pretty clean most of the time. Rachelle, why don't you come over here and cut some of these cookies out for me," she asked as she put some dough out on the counter and began rolling it out. She had enough cookie dough for six-dozen cookies. They would be baking for a while, and assigning Rachelle the job of cutting them out was a perfect task for her industrial personality.

"There's some hot water in the coffeepot if you would like something to warm you up. The tea bags are in the cabinet right above it, Janet. I have one batch of cookies in the oven already, and another cooling, but that's it so far."

"Thanks!" Janet made her way over to the counter and brought three mugs down, making tea for her and Riley and hot cocoa for Rachelle. "Do you like marshmallows in your cocoa, Rachelle?"

"Oh yes! Thank you very much," Rachelle seriously said as she began cutting out snowmen faces and stars. Riley and Shirley had been coaching Rachelle on her manners, and having Janet over was a perfect opportunity for her to show off her newfound "charm." Rachelle was very proud of herself and enjoyed the fact that Janet treated her like an adult rather than a child.

The oven buzzer went off, and Riley changed out one cookie sheet with another, setting the newly baked cookies on the stovetop to cool. It was the paradigm of an efficient assembly line that Riley had learned to manage from her mom, maximizing the amount of cookies baked per hour. Riley didn't really enjoy baking. What she enjoyed was decorating the cookies, so getting the chore of making them over as quickly as possible was the primary goal.

"Here you go," Janet said as she set Riley's tea down next her, then placed Rachelle's cocoa on the kitchen table for her to enjoy away from the hot cookie sheet. "What would you like for me to do, Riley?"

"You can start mixing up the frosting and putting the sprinkles and candy toppings on the table so we are all ready to decorate." Riley had one batch already cooled and ready for decorating and used a spatula to remove them from the baking sheet to place them on a large plate for the table. After Riley moved the cookies, Rachelle and Janet were nearly set.

As Janet finished gathering the necessary supplies and mixing up the white frosting, she moved the candy decorations from the counter to the table within easy reach of Rachelle's station. The girls sat down together and began working on the cookies.

Kevin walked into a kitchen filled with the sweet aroma of homemade cookies, the girlish laughter piquing his curiosity as to the activities going on down the hall. He had been studying in his dad's office all morning and into the afternoon. His belly was talking to him.

He walked to the refrigerator, holding the door open as he surveyed its contents for something appetizing. Janet's demeanor immediately changed when Kevin entered the room, and she became quiet and reserved in his presence.

"What's to eat around here, Riley?" he asked as he turned and stealthily stole a handful of cookie dough from the bowl.

"Don't eat that, Kevin!" Riley protested, moving the bowl out of reach. "There's the pork and sweet potato stew we had for dinner last night, and some stuff for sandwiches in the top drawer. Take your pick, but if you touch my cookies again, you're dead meat."

"Janet, my sister isn't always this mean to me; just so you know," he teased, smiling at her. Janet was cute, and he enjoyed it when she came over. Riley threw a playful punch at Kevin, hitting him square in the gut as she moved past him. "Now that's sisterly love for you!" he declared.

Riley moved to take another batch of cookies out of the oven and placed another dozen in, careful to remember to set the timer. "Are you going on the hayride with us tomorrow night, Kevin?" she asked. Riley had a feeling that Janet was a little sweet on her brother and really asked this question for her benefit.

"Dylan was telling me about it on our trip to KC yesterday," he told them as he reached for the stew. "I promised him I'd help load the straw and drive his truck behind the tractor when he brought it into town."

Putting a pan on the stove to warm up the stew, he took the opportunity to see if the girls knew anything about the murder. He already knew Dylan didn't have any information, but his sister, and Janet for that matter, were much more social and in tune with the happenings of the kids at school.

"Did you hear the new information that's out about the murder case?"

Riley just looked at him, wondering what he was about.

Janet piped up, though. "Yes, I heard that she was a student in the culinary department of Johnson County Community College. She had just been accepted."

"I hadn't heard that," Riley said. "I do know that Lance knew her, though. He was pretty upset that she died."

This was news to Kevin. Very disturbing news. "How did Lance know her?" he carefully asked, not wanting to reveal the alarm he felt.

He had warned Riley to stay away from Lance Meton, and obviously she didn't care to obey his wishes. They would have to have a little discussion about that later tonight, he thought. For now, though, he needed to keep his emotions under control and get as much information as possible.

Riley didn't immediately answer Kevin. Standing there with a spatula in her hand, she shrugged her shoulders and turned back to the cookies.

Kevin and Janet looked at each other, wondering what details Riley was hiding from them. When it looked as if Riley wasn't going to volunteer any more information, Kevin pressed her. "How did Lance know her, Riley?" he asked again, his tone much more serious.

"It's not really my information to tell, Kevin. If you want to know, you will have to ask Lance." Riley was good at sparing with words, but she was not a gossip, and she wouldn't divulge information that was given in confidence. She was just beginning to get to know Lance, and despite the opinions and warnings of her friends, she saw a lot of good things in him. Maybe things others chose to overlook by labeling him according to his appearance. She felt defensive by this sudden confrontation from Kevin and wondered at its source.

"Why are you asking me these things, Kevin? Has Dad said something to you about the case?"

"You know he doesn't discuss the cases he's working on, Riley." A sudden anger flashed across his face, and he struggled to control it. He turned back to the refrigerator and made like he was looking for something else to eat. The stew that he put on the stove was beginning to boil, but he didn't notice it.

"Riley." Janet challenged her in a soft protest about the lack of information. Out of concern she continued, hoping she wasn't pushing their friendship too far. "Can you tell us how he came to talk to you about it?"

Since Rachelle was at the table helping Janet, Riley had reclaimed the job of cookie-cutter-outer. She stopped what she was doing and saw that the stew was about to boil over.

"Kevin!" she shrieked, pointing to the boiling pot.

Kevin jumped and turned the burner off, placing the pot on the back of the stove before turning back to his sister.

Riley could tell he wasn't going to let it go. Tenaciousness was one of his stronger characteristics, and there were times it was not an admirable quality. This happened to be one of them.

"Really, Kevin. I don't see how it's any of your business."

Evasive tactics were a specialty of Riley's. Kevin was prepared and quietly, with great self-control, he said, "You have to understand, Riley, that if he knows something about what happened, he could help bring in the killer. We both know something funny is going on. I for one would like to see the person who did it caught and put behind bars. Don't you think that young woman's mother wants the same thing?"

Bingo. Kevin hit the chord that would make her sing. He saw it on her face, and as she turned to Rachelle, he saw the tears welling up. Janet stood up and came over to her. Looking into her eyes, she continued prompting Riley.

"You can trust us, Riley. We don't mean to hurt Lance. The goal here is to get a killer off our streets."

"What makes you think Lance did it?" Riley flashed.

"I didn't say that, Riley, and you know it," Janet said. "I just think Lance might know something. Maybe he's afraid to tell anyone."

Conflict swelled in Riley's eyes as she looked from Janet back to Kevin. They were the two people she fully trusted in this world. If she couldn't tell them, she couldn't tell anyone.

"I can't tell you everything. What I can tell you is that Lance didn't do it and that he might suspect the person who did."

Stunned, Kevin's immediate reaction was to protect Riley. "I don't want you near him until this killer is caught, Riley. You understand me?"

"Kiss off, Kevin. Who do you think you are, telling me who I will and won't spend time with?" Getting into his face, she challenged his ability to control her. "I'll do whatever I please," she stated with a sudden calmness that unsettled Kevin further.

Janet had never seen Riley and Kevin at each other before, and it was an uncomfortable moment for her. She didn't know what to do or say, so she stayed quiet, watching them draw their battle lines.

With Rachelle forgotten and anger filling the air, Rachelle slipped unnoticed out of her chair and into the little storage room near the back of the kitchen. She quietly closed the door and waited for the storm to blow over.

"What if he comes after you, Riley?" Kevin asked with complete seriousness. "What if this killer suspects Lance knows something, sees you with him, and uses you to get to him?"

"Get real, Kevin. You watch too much TV." She rolled her eyes.

"Promise me you will stay away from him, or I'll tell Dad everything," he threatened.

"You'll probably do that anyway!"

"Promise, Riley," he warned.

Riley knew defeat when she saw it, and she hated him for it at this very moment. She knew that if Dad found out, she would be banned from seeing Lance again anyway. Either way, it was a dead issue.

"Riley." Kevin wanted her to verbally respond, and he wasn't about to let it go until she did. He knew his sister. Even if she did promise, he would need to keep an eye on her. Not because she would say it as an untruth, but because she felt the sting of his protectiveness so acutely. As her twin brother, Kevin was always trying to divert trouble from her life. Lance wasn't the first guy that he discouraged from spending time with her. She was a beautiful, talented woman who trusted people too quickly and rarely saw anything but good in others. He had hoped Janet would help her develop a keener sense of character in others, as she seemed to be able to read people well.

"Yes, Kevin. I will stay away from him until the killer is caught." Tears cascaded down her cheeks.

Janet put her arms around Riley's shoulders, giving her a big hug as Kevin took his stew and left the room. He felt bad about what just happened, but his sister was too important to him to let it go. Sometimes being the big brother also meant being the bad guy, he reasoned as he walked back down the hall to the study. The question now was what should he do with the information he had just received?

***

"Matt!" Stuart greeted his long-term friend on the phone. "Hey, old buddy! How's business in Chicago these days?"

"Stuart, you old dog!" Matt threw back at him. They had been friends since the academy, and he hadn't heard from Stuart since he left Chicago and accepted the detective position in Sweetwater, Missouri. "Merry Christmas!"

"Merry Christmas to you too, Matt!" he said. "How's the wife and kids doing?"

"Jane is out finishing up some shopping for the kids. The boys are on their Xbox, learning life lessons on *Fable II*. They've somehow discovered that kids are expensive and are now declaring they are never getting married and having kids!"

"What a riot, Matt!" Stuart laughed. "Christmas is only a week away. What are you getting June this year?" Stuart was stumped on what to get Shirley, and he needed some ideas. He was hoping Jane would be home to help him out.

"She took me shopping with her a few weeks ago and picked out her own present this year," Matt said. "I just carried the checkbook. How's the job going?"

"I wanted to talk to you about that, Matt. See if you could give me some sage advice."

"Shoot, buddy. Give me the details."

"A hunter found a body on a low-maintenance road out near a cornfield. Execution-style killing. The bullet casing had some interesting markings, making me think that the gun had been altered somehow to accommodate the killer, or maybe just a special order gun from a European manufacturer. The girl wasn't from the area."

"Did you run a ballistics background on the casing to see if you found a match?"

"We're a small town, Matt, with limited resources."

"Send it my way, Stuart. I'll handle it for you."

"I have something else I want to run by you. The sheriff here, he's pretty much told me that I can't interview anyone under the age of eighteen for the murder investigation. I have reason to believe that the kids know something, but if I cross him on this, I'm afraid he could sabotage the case somehow. I'm the new man on the team, remember. It's easier to make enemies than to make friends in this town."

"Do you suspect the sheriff is a bad apple?"

"I don't really know what to think. I'm not used to a superior limiting a murder investigation. The deputy sheriff, Hank Lawson, is a pretty strange character too. Real friendly, real superficial. I catch him out around the high school a lot, talking with the kids, in the parking lot after school, those kinds of things. It's more a gut feeling than anything I can put my finger on, if you know what I mean."

"Gut feelings never lie," Matt said. "I'd advise you to keep information tight, Stuart. You are under no obligation to reveal details until you have them nailed down. Small towns have their share of secrets, and it's an easy place for someone to lay low and hide if he needs to, even pose as an upstanding citizen. We've both seen it before."

Stuart knew he was referring to the BTK killer that posed as an upstanding, Sunday school-teaching leader in his community, all the while seeking out young women to bind, torture, and kill when the mood struck him. It went on for years before he was finally caught. Stuart hoped Sweetwater, Missouri wasn't harboring a monster in the shadows, but he was beginning to wonder.

15

Neil Lemoine stood outside *his* house. He had a right to be there. He owned it. No judge was going to tell him how to live *his* life and no judge was going to keep him from being the man of *his* house. He had been drinking since 9 a.m. that morning and held a half empty bottle of Jack Daniels in his left hand as he closed the door to his truck and staggered toward the front door. He had his great, great-granddaddy's loaded pistol in his right hand. It was a pistol used in the army during the Civil War. The pistol was still in mint condition and unlike Neil Lemoine, it was the pride of the family. He planned to use it if necessary. No one was going to tell him he couldn't see his kids. No one was going to tell him he couldn't see his wife. Time was ticking. He had an agenda and he needed to act now.

Neil had grown up with his older brother, Shaun, running wild through the timbered river bluffs of Missouri. Their pappy was a mean drunk, a two-bit gambler and the best mechanic in the state. He had a sixth sense when it came to engines and even with two-sheets to the wind could out work any man in six counties. He was also a man who taught his boys how to hunt, fish and live off the land. Shaun, being the older and favored child, took to his pappy's teachin' like a cougar cub takes to fresh meat. It was instinctual for him, a gift that bloomed under his pappy's tutelage. Neil had a harder time, and never quite met his pappy's approval. He was a good marksman but never could bring himself to kill a livin' thing. He took many a beatin' for it, too.

"Audrey, get in here!" Neil took a swig of the whiskey as he walked from the front door into the living room. Toys were everywhere. *This place is a pig-sty.* Audrey was nowhere to be seen. She was here somewhere, though. He stood at the foot of the staircase and listened. The wind blew and the old house groaned. It had a lot of character, and memories.

He had inherited the house he grew up in when his pappy died at the ripe old age of thirty-five. An ice storm had been raging for hours. The fire in the wood stove was burnin' low for lack of fuel, but the drink kept his pappy from feeling the cold. No one really knew for sure why he did it, but the old man got up from his chair and walked out the front door in nothin' but a union suit. The sheriff found him two days later, after the ice storm was over, frozen. He had fallen down into a muddy ravine. At least that was the story the town folk knew. Shaun knew the truth of it. Neil didn't ask. What was done was done.

Shaun had left for the army not long after the funeral while Neil took over the family business and home. They were both too young for the responsibility they assumed but that's just how things were. You just did it because you had to, not because you wanted to. Shaun wrote letters occasionally, at one point sharin' that he had been accepted into the Special Forces. Not long after that the letters stopped. Neil married Audrey. Life moved on.

A few months back Shaun just showed up in the middle of the night. Scared the hell out of him. He'd changed: lost a lot of weight, new spade tattoo on his arm, had a coldness to him, an emptiness to his eyes. Asked Neil if he remembered Charlie Joe and if he ever talked to her-if he knew her parents. Of course, Neil knew who they were. Hell, Shaun knew them, too. They'd all grown up together, why wouldn't he know them?

"No, Neil. I mean do you know who her biological parents are?"

"No. Why would I? Charlie Joe doesn't even know that information. Audrey and CJ are best friends. I know that she's been lookin' for 'em. Don't know she's found 'em yet."

"I know who they are, little brother, and I have some unpleasant business to do here in Black Horse. Some things have already been put into motion in Sweetwater, but I need to take care of a problem here, too. Once I'm done here, I'm moving back over to Sweetwater to finish the job."

"I'm not sure I understand what you mean, Shaun."

"The less you know, the better. Don't ask questions. Do what you are told and everything will be ok. You are going to pack your family and leave town. I'm not asking. I'm telling." Shaun's eyes were cold. Dead. A chill had run down Neil's spine just looking at his brother. He wasn't the same person Neil had known as a boy, but he'd changed the night their pappy died.

Neil knew better than to argue with his older brother. Like their pappy, he had a violent streak in him and more than once, Neil had witnessed Shaun in action. The difference between their pappy and Shaun was that Shaun never let his anger get out of control. Fights in school always ended with Shaun still standing. Some people believed that Shaun never felt pain—that that was what made him so dangerous, and deadly. Neil believed it, too. He'd seen too many instances where their pappy had beaten Shaun and Shaun just took the hits. He never cried. He just got back up and took another hit. Neil would beg him to stay down, knowin' that their pappy would quit hittin' Shaun if he would just stay down.

"Ok, Shaun. Where do I go? What am I going to do for a living?"

"I'm having a truck delivered tomorrow. In one week the house will be cleaned out. Drive your family to Saint Louis and wait for me there. I'll be in touch."

That's all that was said that chilly, dark November night. He'd left five thousand dollars in an envelope on the table before walking out the door. Shaun never said why, he just said to get out. Neil had loaded his tools immediately. When he started on the furniture in the house, Audrey went ballistic. That's when all the trouble started and out of frustration, he hit her. It had left a pretty deep bruise. It didn't help that she cut her head on the corner when she fell. Blood was everywhere. He didn't mean to hurt her. He couldn't tell anyone what was going on because he didn't understand it himself. CJ had taken pictures. In court, he over-reacted. Now, he was flat out desperate. They had to leave today. All of them. He couldn't take 'no' for answer.

"Audrey? Get your skinny ass down here. I ain't waitin' any longer!" He sat the Jack Daniel's on the bottom step of the staircase and started up the stairs.

Outside, a truck came to a stop and Neil could hear the engine shut off. Someone else was here.

16

Blackhorse, Missouri

Charlie Joe could hear Neil Lemoine yelling from inside the house as she turned off the engine to her truck and quietly walked up onto the porch of their home. She could tell that he was looking for Audrey and the kids. She could see his shadow just inside the door, at the foot of the staircase.

Audrey Lemoine had called CJ from the upstairs bedroom and told her that her husband, Neil, was on the main floor with a gun. They had all grown up together, and CJ was confident that Neil would not use it on her. Neil didn't have the heart to hurt a squirrel, let alone a person. She remembered him coming to school with dark purple bruises on his face and arms. *No one dared ask about them, but everyone knew. Neil had a gentle heart like his mother. He wasn't like his pappy and he paid the price for it at home.*

"Neil! You put that gun down, you hear?" CJ said as she opened the front door just a crack. She knew he wasn't a killer, but she could tell he was drunk and that made him unpredictable. It was best to use a little caution. Talking loudly would allow Audrey to hear what was going on, and give her some warning if things went south. CJ knew the inside of the house pretty well. The kids and Audrey could climb out onto the roof of the porch and jump down. The timberline wasn't far off and they could all hide there if necessary.

Neil turned towards CJ. The bottle sat at the foot of the stairs. The pistol hung loosely in his right hand. He stood his ground.

"Welcome home, Charlie Joe! We're havin' a party and you're invited!" Neil brought the gun up level with her face. "Come on in."

Audrey peeked her head around the corner at the top of the stairs. Neil turned and saw her. "Come on down, Audrey. Bring the kids with you." He kept the gun on CJ.

"What's going on, Neil. You can't keep everyone hostage forever." CJ was stalling for time. She needed to formulate a plan to get them out of the house safely. "What's your plan, Neil?"

"My plan is to put my family in that truck outside and take them out of this god-forsaken town. We are leavin' together. All of us. Not you, CJ. You're stayin' put."

"Audrey's made it clear she and the kids don't want to leave, Neil. You can't keep them hostage forever. She wants to stay here. This is her home."

"Her home is with me! Isn't that right, Audrey? Why you always pokin' your nose where it don't belong, CJ?"

Audrey stayed at the top of the stairs. She had dialed Jeremiah's cell phone but he wasn't answering. His voicemail turned on. She let the conversation play out. Maybe Jeremiah would check his messages and figure out what was going on. This was the plan that CJ and Audrey had made in case a situation just like this happened. Jeremiah's phone number was on speed dial. Seeing the silver flip phone in her hand, CJ knew exactly what Audrey was doing, and nodded to her, letting her know everything was going to be just fine.

"Neil, put the gun down. Tell me what's going on. It's not like you to want to just up and leave everything. This is your home. Your pappy left it to you. Where are you going to go?" CJ was stalling. She needed time to think. Neil was too big for her to try to overpower, and no one knew she was here. No back up. No help on the way. Not unless Jeremiah picked up his phone.

"That's none of your business, CJ. Time is tickin' and we've got to go. Audrey, I'm going to give you until the count of three to get down here or I shoot Charlie Joe. One..." Neil cocked the trigger, still pointing it at Charlie Joe. The gun hadn't been fired in years, but it was definitely loaded—and potentially deadly.

Charlie Joe was starting to sweat. Things were getting out of hand quickly. She hadn't expected Neil to be so aggressive, but his drinking had made him bolder. It was out of character for him.

"Two..." Neil was taking aim. Audrey was standing at the top of the stairs.

"Stop it, Neil. Stop it right now!" Audrey was putting on a brave front in the midst of ice-cold fear. "I'm coming down. Put the gun down."

Neil kept the gun leveled on CJ. A smile crept across his face. He moved next to CJ, the gun still pointed at her. "Put the kids in the truck, Audrey."

CJ nodded to her. "Go ahead, Audrey. I'll be ok. Neil won't hurt me."

Audrey pushed the two kids past Neil and CJ and then stepped out onto the porch. "Who's coming up the road, Neil?"

A black two-door sports car quietly eased up the narrow driveway, effectively blocking any other vehicles from coming or going. Neil lowered the gun. His face went pale.

"Who is it, Neil?" CJ could tell something bad was going on. "Neil, are you in trouble?"

Shaun stepped out of the car.

This is bad, thought CJ. *This is very, very bad.*

17

Blackhorse, Missouri

Shaun strode confidently towards the house. The moving truck was still in the drive, so obviously Neil didn't have the balls to get his family out. *Typical.* Shaun sighed. *I've always had to be the one to do the dirty work. My little brother can't do anything right. Nothing's changed in all these years.*

A woman with two kids stood on the porch. Although he had never met them, he guessed they were Neil's family. "Where's my brother?"

Neil stepped through the front door out onto the porch. The pistol hung at his side again. His stomach was instantly tied in knots and he felt sick. "I tried to get my family out of town, but Audrey wouldn't leave. The police got involved. I was arrested. The judge ordered me to go to anger management classes. Skipping town now puts me in violation of the court order and I would become a wanted man. I tried, Shaun. I really tried."

"I know you did, little brother. You always *try.* Your problem is that you never *do.*" Shaun put his hand on Neil's shoulder as he spoke and looked him straight in the eyes. "I'm here to fix the problem."

Charlie Joe stepped out onto the porch. "And what problem are you set on fixing this time, Shaun?"

"Well, well, well...." Shaun was truly surprised and pleased at seeing Charlie Joe. "If it isn't the infamous Charlie Joe. I've been looking forward to seeing you again for quite some time." Shaun gave that wicked half smile he always did right before something bad was about to happen. He nodded his head to CJ and turned to Neil. "Take CJ and put her in her truck. Drive her out to our hunting cabin. I'll follow you in my car."

No one but Neil knew anything about a hunting cabin. That was where they skinned deer, harvested meat off the carcass and holed up during long hunting trips. It was very remote. No one had been out there in years. It was unlikely that the off-road trail to the cabin was still accessible, let alone easily found; but maybe that was the point. Shaun didn't want Charlie Joe found.

"Shaun, we don't want to take CJ there. Whatever's going on, let's leave her out of this." The pistol shook in Neil's hand as he spoke. Jack Daniel's was flowing pretty heavily in his veins, and his courage was coming back. Shaun could smell it on his breath and knew exactly what was going on in Neil's mind.

"I wasn't asking you, Neil. I was telling you." Shaun stepped right into Neil's face as he spoke. He towered over Neil by a good six inches and although their body mass was about the same, Shaun clearly was more lithe of limb.

Neil brought the gun up to his waist. It was still cocked, loaded and very dangerous. He pointed into his brother's abdomen. "I'm not doing it, Shaun. You're not goin' to hurt Charlie Joe. What we have here is a family matter. We'll deal with it between us."

***

An instant was all it took. They stood so close together it was hard to tell what really happened right away. All Charlie Joe could see was what appeared to be two brothers dancing in slow motion. A gun went off. Blood began to pool on the floorboards of their pappy's front porch. Violence still reigned supreme in the home. Someone was hurt badly. Audrey screamed.

Shaun let Neil drop to the floor. He wiped his bloody hands on his jeans and grabbed ahold of Charlie Joe's arm, dragging her towards the car kicking and screaming. He was not going to take her without a fight. CJ turned back and saw Audrey on the front porch bent over Neil, hysterical. The kids were at the front door, watching it all. Taking it all in.

"Call Jeremiah, Audrey!" Charlie Joe turned and hit Shaun as hard as she could to try to break free.

The anger was etched all over his face as he squeezed her arm tight, pulled her closer to him and punched her full in the face.

All Charlie Joe saw was a black spade tattoo, coming fast and hard—then everything went black.

18

Blackhorse, Missouri

Jeremiah had felt his cell phone vibrate in his front chest pocket, but he was on the landline with Sheriff Will Langdon and Detective Stuart Riedel. The cell phone would have to wait.

"Where did you say you found the body?" Murders didn't happen just every day in this area of the state. Sheriff Langdon and Detective Riedel had called to see if they could get another set of eyes on the case; someone not from Sweetwater. Someone they both could trust. Jeremiah and Sheriff Langdon had been friends for a very long time. Detective Riedel seemed to be a good man. From the gossip Jeremiah had heard, Detective Riedel was the kind of man you could trust.

"Near the Browning place off of Highway 65. An out of town hunter came across it in the timber at the top of a ravine on the edge of a field." Sheriff Will Langdon was trying to provide as much detail as possible. "Detective Riedel just got a call back from the US Marshall's office. His friend Matthew Johnson ran ballistics on the bullet extracted from a nearby tree. It was a hallow point, 0.38 caliber. Close range execution. The casing and bullet itself have unusual rotation marks that match those of a case tied to a Mexican drug lord named Mombasa. Interestingly enough, he was released from jail a few months ago."

Jeremiah took this information in as he considered how he could help Sheriff Will Langdon. Nothing unusual was happening in his county; at least nothing that he was immediately aware of at the time. Hunters were still plentiful in the area as bow season remained open. They provided a nice flow of income for the area hotels and restaurants, and some farmers had opened their land for hunting at a small price. There were several areas in his county around two different lakes that rented rough cabins by the month. Some of the cabins were owned by families going back generations, and were rarely used. They would provide a nice hide out for someone needing to lay low for a while.

"Do you have any reason to believe that Mombasa could still be in the area?" Jeremiah could send a car out to drive around the cabin sites, see if there was any unusual activity going on. The cell phone in his pocket vibrated again. He pulled it out and turned it off. Without looking at it, he set it on the desk in front of him.

"My experience with this criminal is that he doesn't stay in one place long," Stuart Riedel said. "At one time, he worked with another man that we only know as Spade. He's a ruthless killer and extremely hard to track. We have no idea what he looks like, or who he is, but we do know one thing: he likes to kill. If there is a drug ring in the area, it's likely that Mombasa is involved. Having said that, I'm afraid that Spade is also involved in some capacity and that this is not the only killing we are going to see."

***

Charlie Joe's head was pounding. Her right eye was swollen shut and she could taste blood in her mouth. She felt terribly cold, and the smell of damp mold permeated the air. It was dark and she could hear the dripping of water somewhere behind her. Her hands were tied above her head and her fingers were numb. She tried to move the joints in her fingers, stretching and pulling against the nylon rope, testing the knots and tightness of her bindings. Freeing herself was not going to be easy.

Looking around with her one good eye, she could tell she was either underground, or in a cave somewhere. She strained to hear any noise from the outside, but all she heard was the wind gently rustling dead leaves in nearby trees. A distant light played against the rock walls and grew brighter as it grew nearer. Heavy footsteps carried the torch closer.

Shaun Lemoine's muddy boots stopped inches from her face. He crouched onto his heels, as he looked her over. "Charlie Joe Bingham."

It was a statement. His affect was flat, no emotion: the flashlight shining in her face.

"Shaun, what's going on? Why are you going this?"

"You have no idea do you CJ?"

"Seriously, Shaun. I was trying to help your brother: help Audrey and the kids. That's what the Bingham's do. We help people. Perhaps you've forgotten that since you've been gone."

"Your people never did anything but cause trouble, Charlie Joe. That's what black people do; they cause trouble. You learned well, didn't you?"

"You have a short, and very ungrateful memory, Shaun. My parents tried to treat you and Neil right growing up. They brought you food and took care of your momma—took her in, protected her while they could."

"My momma didn't need protecting."

"I remember the bruises, Shaun. The broken teeth. Your momma took more than one hard beating before my pappy found her in the back woods. She tried to run, to hide from your pappy. I remember the day your pappy came for her. You were there in the truck. You heard him yelling on our front lawn."

Shaun stood and stepped away from Charlie Joe. She could hear a scrapping sound, the light bobbed a bit then settled back on her face. The nylon rope was cutting into her skin, and a small trickle of blood ran down her forearm. Charlie Joe remembered Mrs. Lemoine stepping out on the porch and facing Mr. Lemoine that day. She looked broken, fragile, and resigned. The memory of her opening the passenger door and stepping into the cab of the truck next to Shaun is the last memory Charlie Joe held of Shaun's momma. No one ever saw her again after that; she just disappeared. Gone.

"What happened to your momma that day, Shaun?"

"Your parents should have let her die, Charlie Joe. That was a fatal mistake they made; they tried to help when they should have kept their noses out of our family business. Letting her die would have been the merciful thing to do. Instead, they just caused her more pain."

"Did you watch your pappy kill her?" Charlie Joe already knew the answer, although she didn't have proof. No one did. There were only quiet whispers that followed Shaun and Neil like a dark shadow through the rest of their childhood. Speculation on what happened. No charges were ever filed. The investigation, if you could call it that, went cold after the first few weeks. Seven years later, Mr. Lemoine was found frozen with a broken neck in a nearby ravine. Shaun left and Neil took over the family business.

"Your parents, CJ. You don't know who they really are, do you?"

Shaun was baiting her, trying to find that deep, painful spot in her emotions. Everyone in town knew that CJ wanted to know her birth parents. For some reason, right now, CJ really didn't care. At this moment, it didn't matter to her anymore. Her adoptive parents, a black Christian couple, had taught her what was important in life. They gave her love, and security; things some white folks never gave their kids. She refused to answer him, instead, she stared into the light, waiting.

"Charlie Joe, you are here in this shit-hole, tied up because someone has to pay for the sins of your real parents. Let me explain some things then I'll tell you what's going to happen. First, your biological parents, your pappy, he used to be a US Marshall. We had a run in a few years ago. He caused me some trouble. It took some time, but I found him and you know what? He lives right next door to you in Sweetwater, Missouri. Your adoptive parents, well their sins were getting into my family business. Bad things happen when you stick your nose where it doesn't belong and my momma suffered because of it."

Shaun paused, watching Charlie Joe.

"We live in a small town, Shaun. Caring about neighbors is what we do." Charlie Joe knew that a new detective had moved into Sweetwater with his family. Jeremiah and Sheriff Will Langdon were friends.

Jeremiah had mentioned it in passing a while back. She let this knowledge, and the pain that her biological family lived so close without her knowing, hang in the air between them.

"I find it hard to believe that you knew about Detective Riedel being your pappy, CJ. You're doing a fine job of covering up your surprise but I assure you, it's true. I'm an information specialist, Charlie Joe. I know things. People pay me very well for information, but they pay me even better for discretion and disposal; if you know what I mean." Shaun stood and the light bean dropped to the floor. Charlie Joe could see his outline above her. The cold was beginning to creep into her bones and the pain in her head and wrists was increasing as they talked. She felt sleepy and struggled to stay awake. He stepped towards her and crouched beside her head. "I'm going to have some serious fun over the next couple of hours, Charlie Joe. You see, I've got some business to do in the area, but when I'm done I'm going on a hunt, a hunt that I've been dreaming of *for years*. I'm going to bait and hunt Detective Riedel and his family: your family. When I'm done, I'm coming back here, to see you. Just so you can think about it, I'm going to describe what's going to happen when I come back. I'm going to take your clothes off and cut you loose. I'll give you a fifteen-minute head start, and then I'm going to begin tracking you like a wild animal. It will be great fun, Charlie Joe, a game of wits and survival. In the end, you'll be dead, just like my momma. We'll play out that scenario and you'll finally know how she died."

19

Sweetwater, Missouri

Peace had been restored to the Riedel home in the form of cell phones for both Kevin and Riley. Stuart and Shirley had already activated the phones and decided that an early present would help maintain the sanity of the house during the days dwindling toward Christmas.

Riley was sitting on her bed in her room, reading the manual and setting up voice mail when Rachelle knocked on the door. She opened it a crack and peeked in at her sister before daring to enter.

"Come on in, Munchkin." Patting the edge of the bed, Riley invited Rachelle to join her.

"Can I see your new phone?" she softly asked, eyes full of wonder.

"Sure," Riley agreed, handing it to her as she climbed up on the queen-sized mattress of the antique four-poster bed. Riley loved antique furniture and would beg her parents to take her to auctions when they lived in Illinois. Since moving to Missouri, she had not had the opportunity to find any antique haunts in the area, although she knew this part of the United States was replete with opportunities to go antiquing.

Her favorite piece was a white-gold band that she had found at an auction a few years back. The wife had died, and the husband was selling everything so he could move into an assisted living facility. She had talked with the elderly gentleman for some time while her parents perused the numerous items for sale and had learned how he had met his bride.

Rachelle loved to hear Riley recount the story to her and would often come into her room, open Riley's jewelry box to retrieve the ring, and ask for the "ol' man's legend" to be told. Riley had started wearing the ring recently, even though it was a little too big. Riley took a break from reading the phone manual and spun the ring on her finger recounting the story of the ring in her mind as she watched Rachelle play with the phone.

The ring had belonged to the daughter of a wealthy businessman. His own wife had died on the train from the flu during a long and difficult move across Ohio into Illinois. Since the conductor was not allowed to carry a body across state lines without written authorization, the train had stopped just outside Illinois long enough for the train crew to dig a grave. A few words were said over the body. Then the businessman and his young daughter were placed back on the train to continue their journey.

Once they reached their destination in Illinois, the wealthy businessman suddenly became ill. As his health continued to fail, he grew more and more concerned about his daughter. He accepted a partnership in his business, with the understanding that if he died, as he instinctively knew he would, the partner would raise his little girl as his own. Three days after the papers were signed and the partnership sealed, the wealthy businessman died.

The business partner had been the old man's own father, and the little girl, orphaned by hardship, adopted through a partnership, grew up to become his wife. Providence, the old man believed, had brought her across the country to win his heart.

"Sometimes people can't take care of their babies, can they?" Rachelle asked as she longingly held the new phone in her hands.

"Sometimes things happen that are out of our control, Rachelle. We have to learn to make the best of what comes our way." Rachelle had told Riley the story of the ring many times, but this question had never come up before.

"Is that why people give up their baby for adoption?" Riley looked at her sister with complete openness.

"That's a strange thing to ask." Riley wasn't sure where Rachelle was getting ideas about adoption. "I thought you were asking about the old man that I got the ring from again. Who do you know that was adopted?"

"I know the ring-story, Riley," Rachelle scoffed as she gave her sister a dirty look. "Can I call someone?" Rachelle asked.

"Not now, Rachelle. I want to figure it out first. It's not a toy."

"I know that!" she responded indignantly, hopping off the bed as she spoke. "Are you going to see that boy again?"

"You need to mind your own business," Riley asked her, suddenly defensive.

Rachelle just shrugged her shoulders, dropped the phone on the bed, and walked out of the room.

Riley knew she had promised to not see Lance until the killer was caught, but they both knew that little event might never happen. She would keep her promise, as she was not one to go against her word. *That doesn't mean I can't speak to him*, she thought as she began dialing his number. She'd keep her word, but she'd also do as she pleased. Kevin could keep her from seeing Lance, but he couldn't keep her from caring about him.

"Lance! It's Riley," she said, her voice smiling across the line.

***

Mombasa had asked for a private meeting, and Lance was obliged to come when called. The drug lord had given him an address and said to meet him there that afternoon. Riley had called him just as he was crossing over the Missouri state line.

The sound of her voice gave him a rush, and he was careful to not suggest he was anywhere but home. Focusing on the call rather than on the interview before him, he was able to relax a little and enjoy her company. She was a sweet girl and very innocent. She had her own ideas and a bit of a temper. She had admitted telling Kevin that Lance knew something of the murder and about the ensuing argument that happened. Everything was falling into place just as Lance had planned.

Patience and planning, those were his strengths. He just needed a little more time, and he would be out from under Mombasa and free to pursue Riley in an honorable manner, something he'd never done before. It was all definitely new territory for him, but for her he was willing to try. Although his options at the Salvation Army were limited, he'd shopped there for some different clothes in an effort to attract her. Money was tight, but she was worth it.

"Riley, I have to go now, but I'll call you later, OK?" he said, trying to get off the phone as he got closer to his destination. She sounded disappointed, he thought, but he couldn't talk any longer.

"Have fun tonight with your friends and be nice to your brother," Lance said. "He just cares about you. I'll call you later, I promise," he said, snapping his phone closed and refocusing on the building in front of him.

It looked deserted, except for the white Lincoln parked next to the door. A white Hummer idled next to the Lincoln, giving the meeting he was about to join a new level of seriousness.

Lance entered the warehouse building and walked through a maze of stacked cargo containers to an area that was brightly lit. He could see three people congregated together under the lights. An open crate had been brought in, and parts of its contents were displayed on the lid.

A large man dressed in a camel-colored overcoat stood beside the crate. His hair was freshly cut, and he sported a goatee. Lance recognized this man as Spade, having met him in Wichita for the first time just a few days prior. Another man—Lance couldn't see his face—sat in a chair with his hands tied behind him, wearing jeans and a short-sleeved shirt. As he continued to approach the group, Lance wondered about the man who was sitting. The warehouse was very cold.

"Lance!" Mombasa welcomed him. He was a short man wearing a very expensive gray suit. A red power tie accentuated the delicate line of the suit. Expensive Italian-made shoes peeked out from under cuffed trouser pants, giving the small-framed man a look of leisure. "So glad you could make it today," he said with warmth and deep irony as he stepped forward and greeted him with a handshake that pulled him fully into the circle. The man who was sitting was now behind Lance, so he could not see his face.

Lance acknowledged Spade with a slight nod of his head, while returning Mombasa's firm handshake. "You asked me to come, sir."

Laughter from the two men echoed off the walls.

"Yes! Yes! Of course!" Mombasa said, patting him on the back. "You see, Spade, why I like this boy so? Quite the one for the job at hand, don't you think?"

Spade did not answer but let his gaze fall on the man in the chair behind Lance.

"I don't know what you mean, sir," Lance said, turning to follow Spade's gaze. Instant recognition froze his heart, and his blood ran cold.

The wind had picked up and started to howl through the old windowpanes of the warehouse. The river just to the north humidified the air, putting an extra icy chill to the razor-edge wind as it crept in. Huge crates packed the expanse of the room, creating an organized and detailed maze of shipped goods held for transport. As the holidays were in full swing, the warehouse did a brisk business as a holding destination for goods. The shipping industry would move items that were quick sellers and hold items back for later transport to increase revenue. Underground shipping had become popular with the Mafia, and warehouses were an easy place of business for a drug lord to access, even during high-traffic holiday seasons.

Despite the cold of the warehouse, Lance was developing a bead of sweat on his upper lip. He felt a tremor develop in his hands as he slipped them into the shallow pockets of his light jacket. Lance tried to ward off the mental chill of the room by focusing on Mombasa as he paced in front of him. Hank Lawson sat behind him, obviously having just endured what appeared to be a deadly beating to the head and upper torso.

Mombasa smoked a cigarette and let the ashes fall upon the cement floor unnoticed. He paced a few steps away from the light as if to gain strength from the darkness before speaking.

"Do you know how this man came to be known as Spade?" he asked as he turned back toward them. Lance did not follow the line that he drew in the air toward his quiet associate. Instead, he held Mombasa's gaze with his own, silently quelling his emotions, trying to show a strength he did not truly feel.

Seeing that Lance was unmoved, he continued. "Because he's unmatched in reconnaissance and information-gathering abilities," he bragged as he drew on his cigarette. "He's an expert killer, and he can dispose of a body in such a way as to make it impossible for even a trail-hardened FBI agent to find a trace of DNA." As Mombasa blew out a stream of smoke, Lance envisioned as him a demon angel in human form, gloating over a championed soul at the gates of hell. "Spade's work doesn't come cheap, but he's well worth the price I pay him. He's competent and he never leaves a trace."

Lance reminded himself that the choice he made a year ago, to walk this path, was his alone. It had been a badge of anger and rebellion that he now regretted, and more than anything he wanted to free himself from it. To keep his mind focused, he remembered the plan he had started: let it slip that he knew the killer and hope that Riley's dad would find out, revealing the trail that was unwittingly left by Mombasa.

"Hank," Mombasa yelled, shattering Lance's thoughts. "Tell the young Lance Meton why you think Meretrix's body was left in the open for the police to find."

Lance kept his focus on Mombasa, acutely aware of the lack of response from Officer Lawson. Spade watched every response that Lance gave, using this game of cat and mouse to gauge the young man.

Walking behind Lance to stand at the back of Officer Hank Lawson, Mombasa grabbed his hair and forced his head to an awkward angle, forcing a weak cry from the bloodied victim.

"Hank, tell our friend the plan. The one you decided to change," he hissed into his ear. Throwing his head forward, Mombasa paced around to Lance and stood inches from his face. Lance began counting backward by nines in his mind in an attempt to control his adrenaline. Lance knew Spade was watching him, but his mind fought to dwell on another potential spy in town, someone who might be tracking his moves, someone chained by Mombasa's influence. The longer he stood in the dim light of the warehouse, the more clear the folly of his plan became. By telling Riley he knew the killer, he most assuredly endangered her life as well as his own.

Mombasa's breath reeked of hate. "Meretrix died because she made a mistake. Understand that, Lance. She had to be punished. It was simply a business matter, nothing personal. The body was left as a warning to my soon-to-be-late friend here," he said, nodding to Officer Hank Lawson. "Instead of following orders, he left town. He tried to escape the reach of my influence. As you can see, he underestimated me." Laughing, he stepped back and turned to Spade. "We have an obvious problem that needs to be eliminated. You see, because of Officer Lawson, Detective Riedel has evidence that point directly to me. I need you, Spade, to eliminate this situation and retrieve the bullet and the casing.

"Also, Lance needs to understand for whom he works," Mombasa said. "Please make sure there is no misconception about our alliance he so willingly embraced a year ago. I would hate to see him retire from this wonderful business. Lance has such huge potential." He took one last pull on his dwindling cigarette.

Turning to Lance, he quietly lingered over his thoughts, tossing the still-burning butt toward the edge of the light. Mombasa saw what he perceived as innocence in the boy's face, but his mannerisms in the face of fear belied that impression. *Lance Meton has a deep well of hardness within,* he thought, pondering ways in which to draw him deeper into his inner circle. *Lance could be molded, if I had the right motivator.*

Without speaking another word, Mombasa left the warehouse. Two men who had been standing in the shadows silently joined him as he reached the door, leaving Lance and Spade with a near-unconscious Officer Lawson.

20

Blackhorse, Missouri

Jeremiah had sent two police cruisers out to drive around the local hunting cabins. It was unlikely that the officers would find anything out of the ordinary but given the circumstances it was wise to at least do a preliminary drive by. Sheriff Will Langdon and Detective Riedel had both agreed that the Mexican drug lord was probably long gone. It was unlikely that anyone else working with him was still in the area.

He went back to his office and opened the case on his desk for the Siley's missing tractor. It had been gone now for a couple of weeks, and there was no sign of it anywhere. The case had gone cold, but he had a sneaky suspicion that Charlie Joe knew something about it. He didn't know why he felt that way, but he did, nonetheless. He closed the file and moved it to the side of his desk when Mark Hubbard barged into the room. Mark lived next to Neil Lemoine and the look on his face was one of anger and desperation.

"Where the hell have you been? Shaun is back. Neil is in an ambulance on the way to the hospital. Shaun shot him."

"What?"

"Audrey has been trying to reach you on your cell phone for the last two hours. Charlie Joe. Shaun took her hostage, Jeremiah. He took her!"

21

Riley had promised to meet Janet at her house early, so Kevin dropped her off on his way out to Dylan Forrester's home. Kevin would follow Dylan behind the tractor-trailer, as part of the journey would be on the highway at dusk. Dylan's dad didn't want him on the highway with a slow-moving vehicle without some precaution, and Kevin agreed to fill that bill. The boys would be in town at Janet's house by seven o'clock so everyone could load onto the flatbed and start the caroling tour of the town.

"Amy is riding on the tractor with Dylan, so she'll be coming to town with them," Janet said. "Have you gotten to know Amy very well yet?"

"Honestly, I haven't, Janet," she said as they gathered blankets from Janet's mom's hall closet. As she pulled a blanket out, a small package dropped to the floor, and Riley reached to pick it up. "What's this?"

Janet took it from her hands and turned it over. "I don't know. It's wrapped in brown paper, though, and tied with a string, so it must be expensive. My mom always wraps the expensive presents in this kind of paper. It's a game of hers. The cheaper the gift, the more expensive the wrapping and vice versa." She laughed. "It's so close to Christmas, I wouldn't doubt it's a present for someone."

"We'd better put it back, Janet," Riley said, watching her friend.

Janet was quite intrigued, and Riley could see mischief working behind her eyes. "What if I just took a peek inside?"

"No, Janet, you can't do that," Riley said, taking the package from her friend and returning it to the closet. Closing the door, she stooped to pick up the blankets they had pulled out and started for the front foyer of the Nelsons' home.

Janet stood pouting, watching Riley move the blankets. She was an only child, and her parents were often away on business. She had practically raised herself and thought that if she wanted to know what was in the package, she had a right to open it and see what was inside. She suddenly resented Riley's admonishment but didn't want to spoil the evening.

Riley felt something hard and heavy in the blankets as she tried to pick them up. Pulling a handgun out from the folded blankets, she looked at Janet. "You have a gun in the house?"

"It's my mom's gun. She likes to keep one in the house for protection. Sometimes dad is away on business." Janet took the Smith and Wessen M&P Shield gun from Riley. Her mom had told her about the gun and had taken her to the gun range a few times to teach her how to use it in case an emergency occurred. Despite this experience, Janet didn't like the gun and felt uncomfortable handling it. "It holds 9mm bullets and only weighs 19 ounces. Mom likes it because it's small and fits in her hand well. Mom taught me how to use it, but I don't care for it much. I'm sure that since your dad was an FBI agent that he taught you and Kevin all about guns."

Riley watched Janet handle the gun and admired the fact that she obviously knew what she was doing. She carefully took the gun from Janet and turned it over to look at it. "He taught Kevin, but mom didn't think I needed to know how to handle one so I didn't have to learn. I think it's cool that your mom wanted you to learn about it."

"Be careful. Mom keeps it loaded. You can see that the safety is on, but it's still dangerous. Here, I'll show you how to do it." Janet took the gun from Riley, excited to actually know something that Riley didn't. She turned it over and explained how to click the safety off and load the chamber. "This is how you know the gun is loaded. Once the bullet is in the chamber, it's ready to fire." She then took the bullet out of the chamber and put the safety back on.

Riley watched as Janet put the gun back into the holster and placed it back on the shelf where it had been hidden under the blankets they removed. "I'm a little jealous, Janet. I wouldn't expect that your parents were the type to carry guns."

Janet liked the idea of her friend being a little jealous of her. That didn't happen very often. "We better get moving. The boys are waiting for us," Janet said as she closed the closet door.

***

Kevin pulled into Dylan's driveway at five thirty. It was a little earlier than expected, but he wanted to talk privately with him and knew that Amy would be there soon to join the ride back into town. Parking the blue '68 Mustang next to the truck that Dylan's parents gave him to drive, he reached into the backseat to retrieve his coat when he noticed that Riley had dropped her phone on the floor of the car before getting out at Janet's. He reached down to pick it up and thought for a moment. *She's been too compliant about not seeing Lance. I wonder if she's been talking to him on the phone,* he thought. He scrolled through the phone menu system and found the call logs listed. Dialing a number he didn't recognize, but suspected to be Lance, he waited. The phone rang and rang, but no voice mail activated. He still didn't know who the number rang to, but he was determined to ask Riley about it as soon as the party tonight was over.

Putting the cell phone in the inner pocket of his jacket, he headed toward the front door. Mrs. Forrester, Dylan's mom, answered the door before he got to the porch of the old farmhouse. She was a tall woman of obvious German stock. She loved to cook and loved even more to share her confections with others. As long as Kevin had known the Forrester family, they always had some fresh-baked goods available for an unexpected visitor.

"Kevin! So nice to see you again," she warmly greeted him. "I heard your sister play the piano the other night and was just mesmerized by her talent. What a wonderful gift she has. Dylan is putting his boots on and will be ready in a moment. Why don't you come on in, and I'll give you a piece of homemade cherry pie while you wait."

"Thank you, Mrs. Forrester," he said. "I'd be happy to deprive my best friend of his momma's homemade pie."

Mrs. Forrester was more than pleased as she led him into her warm kitchen. It was a small home, but well kept. Dylan's father was a contract builder by trade and farmed more as a hobby than as an occupation. Because his other job was lucrative, he was able to inject cash into his farming operation that other full-time farmers envied. He had a new tractor and a strong line of Angus cattle wintering in a pasture just north of the home.

Kevin sat down at the small harvest table in the kitchen. Benches lined the table instead of chairs. Dylan had two older brothers who were away at college, so at one point, the kitchen had been a full and thriving beehive of activity. As it was, Dylan was the baby of the family, and Mrs. Forrester was missing the rambunctiousness of her boys.

Dylan came into the kitchen just as she sat a slice of pie down in front of Kevin. "I'm about ready to go, Kevin," he said as he cut a piece of pie for himself and brought it over to the table to join him. Dylan heard Kevin come in the door and noticed he didn't take his coat off before sitting down at the table. This was a pretty good sign that Kevin didn't mean to stay long. They had only known each other since the summer, but Dylan knew Kevin pretty well. He was a young man who worked hard and took care of his own. Dylan held a lot of respect for his friend, even when they were at odds.

Kevin scooped up the last of his pie and stood to put his plate in the kitchen sink, leaving Dylan at the table finishing his piece of pie. Kevin turned to Mrs. Forrester, thanked her for her hospitality, and quietly waited for Dylan.

The boys were soon out at the barn hitching the flatbed trailer up to the John Deere 4020 tractor and loading bales of straw down the center of the trailer for people to sit on. After this task was accomplished, and they were ready to head out, Dylan drove the tractor to the head of the driveway to wait for Amy.

The wind was picking up. It was sure to be a very cold night. There wasn't a cloud in the sky, and in the early hours of dusk, Kevin could already see a star or two blinking in the night canvas.

"Dylan, I want to ask you something in confidence, and I want you to be perfectly honest with me, OK?" Kevin began.

Dylan wasn't sure what this was about. "Ask away," he said.

"You told me when we first met to stay clear of this Lance Meton guy. You said there was something about him that wasn't right, but that you had never actually seen him do anything wrong. As a friend, I want to know everything you know about this guy."

"You know what I know, Kevin. He's a bum, runs with a rough crowd out of Kansas City. I suspect he deals, and I'm pretty sure he's not a user."

"Why do you say that?"

"Look. Lance has been around for a while. His old man is in prison, and his mom works nights. He's a really smart kid, makes everyone in the high school look the idiot when it comes to math. I've seen the guy memorize an entire page of literature in minutes. It's creepy. He never missed a day of school until last year. There was an after-school party at a club up in Kansas City. The club was new and targeted kids who were too young to drink. We all drove up there together on the weekends for a while. It was a cool place to be. Lance started hanging with this chick he met. She was a few years older than him, and I guess because the home girls didn't really put much stock in the geek, this new attention from a very sexy woman made him feel good."

Kevin was listening with rapt attention, but the more he knew about Lance, the more he didn't understand what was really going on. "What do you know about the body that was found, Dylan?"

Unsure what to say, Dylan looked out over the plowed field across from his parents' house. The lights inside the home gave it an inviting warmth, especially since he was sitting outside on a cold metal tractor. Dylan could feel his butt going numb as he stepped off the tractor to stand on the ground for a while. Kevin hopped off the metal fender of the John Deere to join him, still waiting for an answer.

"After Lance met this girl, she started coming back here to meet him. You'd see him in the shadows at postgame parties and such, but he always had people from KC with him. This girl was there as well. He quit being friendly, started missing school, dropped out of debate. Not long after that, he started dressing in black clothes, and you could see tattoo markings on his arms. He got rebellious and just, you know, went off the deep end. About the time that you guys moved to town, Lance started changing again. He doesn't miss school much anymore, and he's starting to wear normal clothes again. I can't say that he still doesn't give me the creeps from time to time, but I think there's been a change, or at least, there had been a change until the body was found.

"I don't know if he killed her or not, but Lance certainly knew her," Dylan said. "She was the girl he met that night in KC."

"You know that my sister has made friends with Lance, don't you, Dylan?"

"Yes," he admitted, not sure how much he should tell Kevin.

Kevin wasn't backing down so easily. "I need to know, Dylan."

"Janet and Lance have been friends for about six years now. Janet doesn't get involved with the people from Kansas City, but from what Amy tells me, Lance has been over to their house when Riley is there. They haven't exactly 'gone out,' but they've had plenty of opportunity to get to know each other.

"Look, Kevin," he said, "Lance isn't all bad. He's just made some stupid decisions along the way. Who hasn't, you know? Your sister has had a positive impact on him, and everyone knows it. I know his family isn't exactly the pillar of the community, but you can't condemn the man for it."

"You still haven't told me why you think he's dealing drugs."

"I don't really think he's that deep into it, Kevin. I suspect what's really going on is that he's moving them. He's not using. He's too smart for that, but if he's moving drugs, he's in contact with some seriously bad dudes."

"You knew this and didn't tell me about it." Kevin was beginning to question his friendship with Dylan.

"I didn't figure it was any of my business. Amy and Janet have been friends for a while. I only knew because Amy tells me what Janet tells her. They didn't go out or do anything that I'm aware of. It's just a friendship that has developed is all."

"Do Janet's folks know she's hanging with a bad crowd?"

"I have no idea what her folks know, Kevin. I'm not the police." He was beginning to feel defensive.

"Why do you suspect he's moving drugs? What do you know that makes you think that?"

Dylan didn't like the way this conversation was heading. He invited Kevin out because he needed the help, not so that he could be interrogated over something he really didn't know anything about. It was all just speculation and gossip anyway. His girlfriend, Amy, liked to talk, and being a social butterfly, she knew things. He didn't know them firsthand and didn't like repeating what he had heard, especially when it could be misconstrued or taken out of context.

"Kevin, I only hear the gossip that comes on the grapevine through Amy. It's not fact, and I certainly haven't personally seen or encountered anything that I can give you as absolute truth. I can promise, though, that if I hear anything or see anything unusual that I'll tell you. Riley is your sister, and that fact alone makes your concern for her important to me. Friends watch out for each other. Deal?"

Kevin appreciated that Dylan recognized his concern, as well as the promise offered. "Thanks, Dylan. I'm worried about her is all. I can't let anything happen to her. Know what I mean?" Riley was his twin, and there were times when he sensed things weren't right with her.

He couldn't explain it, but he certainly wasn't about to ignore it. This happened to be one of those times. Something wasn't right.

Amy's headlights shone over the hill south of the house, and the two boys stood and watched as her car approached Dylan's driveway. She turned in and drove up to park next to Kevin's Mustang. After parking her car, she got out and walked back to where they stood, waiting.

"Hey, Amy," Kevin greeted her.

"All ready to go, boys?" She grinned. Amy was sure this night was going to be a blast and was eager to get things moving.

"I'll get the car and drive behind you," Kevin said. "Go ahead and start heading into town. I'll be caught up with you by the time you reach the highway."

Amy crawled up on the fender of the tractor and waited. Dylan crawled up after her, taking his place behind the wheel and starting the engine. Putting the tractor in second gear, he eased out onto the gravel road and turned back toward town. Kicking the speed up a few notches, Dylan was watchful of any traffic that might happen along the way, being careful to pull closer to the side of the road when approaching hills, as oncoming traffic wouldn't be able to see that he was a slow-moving vehicle. Kevin caught up with them in his Mustang just as they reached the highway and followed them into town with his hazard lights on.

They reached Janet's house right at seven o'clock, and they could see that a nice crowd had gathered to join in the fun. Kevin scanned the group as people emerged from the warmth of the house with their blankets and thermoses filled with hot cocoa. He didn't see Lance, but his gut feeling that something was amiss kept him vigilant.

Dylan counted thirty-one kids on the trailer before starting their route, being watchful that no one fell off or tried jumping off while they were in motion. Kevin took up his position on the trailer as they pulled out, abandoning the follow car, as the route they were taking was mostly in town on well-lit roads. The last of the route was the darkest, taking them past the county cemetery and an old abandoned barn. Kevin and Dylan had driven the route the day before, so Kevin was aware that this stretch was dangerous. They prepared for it by bringing along lanterns to light and place on the back of the trailer during this stretch of the journey.

Two of the houses on the route were fairly close to Janet's, and as soon as the tractor-trailer stopped, the kids piled off. They burst out with "O Come, All Ye Faithful." The O'Malleys came to the door, ecstatic that they were chosen by the high schoolers for caroling. They continued a cappella singing through a short repertoire before making a showy bow and descending upon the trailer for a ride to the next house. Shouts and laughter filled the night air, and as they progressed from house to house, the group became more animated and energized.

Dylan was keeping warm, as heat was blowing back on him from the engine. Amy, riding above the left tire on the cold steel of the fender, was near freezing as they reached the halfway point in their adventure. At the last house, she asked Kevin to trade places with her so she could warm up under blankets on the trailer during the ride back to Janet's house. After lighting the lanterns, Kevin jogged up to the front of the trailer and climbed up onto the fender beside Dylan.

"It's been a fun night, don't you think?" Kevin said as he kept one hand on the back of the tractor seat for balance and tucked the other into the pocket of his coat to keep warm.

Making one last check to make sure everyone was on, Dylan turned back to Kevin. "Yeah, I think so. Everyone seems in good spirits." He pulled away from the curb and kicked the speed up a few gears. The wind was blowing pretty hard from the north, and the stars where as bright as Dylan had ever seen them. Looking up ahead, being aware that a car could come upon them at any time, Dylan was watchful of his surroundings. A bright fire seemed to be burning in the distance next to the road.

"What do you make of that, Kevin?" Dylan asked as he pointed in the direction of the light that had caught his attention. It was a good mile in front of them, but seemed to grow in intensity as they came near.

"Looks like a scarecrow staked to the fence that somebody lit," Dylan suggested as they got closer. "Wrong holiday for that sort of thing."

"Why would somebody do that?" Dylan wondered aloud.

The crowd of high schoolers on the trailer began to notice the fire too. As they approached, they grew quieter, trying to decide what it was they were seeing.

Kevin felt a buzz next to his chest and jumped, forgetting that he carried Riley's phone in his pocket. Reaching in to retrieve it, he answered, thinking it must be Mom or Dad checking to make sure they were all OK.

"Hello?" Kevin said.

A deep voice that Kevin didn't recognize answered with two words: *You're next.* The caller then immediately hung up. Confused, Kevin closed the phone and noticed that Dylan had slowed considerably as he got closer to the fire.

"Kevin, use your phone to call your dad," Dylan ordered. "Do it now."

Not really understanding, Kevin dialed the number before looking up again to see that a man had been staked to the wooden fence that lined the cemetery and set aflame. His body burned in front of them. As Kevin connected with his dad on Riley's phone, the first screams of recognition sounded from the trailer behind them.

22

Blackhorse, Missouri

Cora Mae Vaxter had worked as a waitress since graduating from high school. She hadn't planned to make a career of it, but life happened, and there it was. She enjoyed the people she worked with, and the customers for the most part, were kind to her. It helped that she had a sharp mind and remembered details without writing them down. She could take an order for a party of twenty and get everything correct with the first serving. Memorizing people's preferences was a gift that few waitresses could manage, and she did it with ease, making her a favorite with the regular crowd.

The most joy that she received in life was through her friendships with Audrey Lemoine and Charlie Joe Bingham. It was because of the tight relationship with these two women that Cora Mae felt the freedom to pry and invade their private lives when warranted. It wasn't really an invasion of privacy for her to do a little investigation and to use hard-won knowledge to advance the lives of those she loved. Why, Charlie Joe did that almost every day now in the courtroom and got paid for it. Well, maybe not now, as she had stepped on Judge Winkler's toes and been ordered to do pro bono cases for a while, but all the same, she was out there, doing similar work for the common good.

That's how she justified what she was about to do. "Good morning, Judge Winkler," she cooed as she carried the empty coffeepot back to the coffee machine and proceeded to make a fresh pot for her late-morning customers. Cora Mae took her time, waiting for the judge to settle into his usual spot in the corner before she approached him for his order.

"Will it be the usual today?" she asked as she poured him a cup of decaf coffee and set a clean set of silverware on the table.

"Thank you, Cora Mae," he said as she filled his cup. Judge Winkler's wife had died a few years back. He started coming in twice a day to Big Daddy's Diner shortly after that. "The usual will be fine, but can you give me a couple of slices of bacon on the side today too?"

"Your doctor told you to cut back on the salt, Judge. Bacon won't be good for you, and you know if you go in to see him next week, he'll ask you about it." Cora Mae knew more about her customers than just their orders. She was their friend and sometimes their confidant.

"Just give me the damn bacon. To hell with doctors, Cora Mae. I'm going to die someday anyway. Why not enjoy myself a little before I step into the grave?"

Smiling back at him, Cora Mae walked back to the kitchen and placed his order. Eddie Morton Jr., the owner of the diner and Cora Mae's current boyfriend, was manning the grill. The diner was almost empty this time of day. After placing his order, she took the time to wrap silverware in napkins for the next shift. Thinking on the best way to proceed, she waited for the order to be called up before heading back to the judge's table.

"Here you are, Judge." She placed a steaming plate of hash browns with over-easy eggs and bacon on the side. She then placed a glass of fresh-squeezed orange juice down in front of him. He hadn't ordered the orange juice, but she knew he liked it and would drink it. Seeing he was about to tuck into his breakfast, she slid into the seat across from him.

"Judge, can I ask you a legal question?"

He poured a generous supply of salt over his eggs as he looked over at her. Since he didn't say anything, she felt it was OK to continue.

"I have this relative who is pregnant and thinking about giving the baby up for adoption," she quickly said while she still had the courage to say it. "She's worried that someday the baby will want to know who she is and wonders what legal standings could help her baby find her if it came to that."

"Missouri law is such that all adoption proceedings are closed. They are not public record, meaning you can't just go to the courthouse and access them. A separate index, docket, and minute book is kept so that the original name of the child and the child's natural parents can be known if just cause to open the records can be shown. It's rare that that happens, but if necessary, those records can be opened."

Cora Mae glanced out the window, thinking on what the judge had just told her. How could she show just cause to gain access to those records? Who could she get to help her?

Judge Winkler was no fool. He knew Cora Mae and Charlie Joe Bingham were close friends, and he also knew that Charlie Joe was struggling with some personal matters in her life just now. He could see it in her work with the kids she had been assigned to by the district attorney's office. Young people often struggled with needing to know their heritage. If this was the reason Charlie Joe was having a hard time, well, he felt he needed to do something to help her. He wasn't sure he could do anything for her from a legal standpoint, but as a friend, he could make a call. Cora Mae didn't need to know about it, so he didn't volunteer any information. Instead, he sat across from her, enjoying a hot breakfast on a cold, blustery morning.

Seeing that the judge was enjoying his breakfast, Cora Mae thanked him for his time and excused herself. Satisfied that she had succeeded in gathering information without raising suspicion, she walked back to the kitchen to talk with Eddie.

"Missy Bowers should be here any minute, Eddie. She agreed to take the second shift today, and I'm going to knock off early." Cora Mae hung up her apron and pulled on her coat. Eddie was busy cleaning the grill and didn't look up as he spoke to her.

"That's fine, Cora Mae. I have a little surprise for you, though, if you have a minute." He wiped his hands on a cloth and turned to look at her.

Warning bells began to chime in Cora Mae's brain as Eddie walked past her and into his office. Eddie wasn't a man given to "surprises," and his definition of one had her worried. He came back out of the office and handed her a sealed envelope.

"What's this, Eddie?"

"I overheard you and Audrey talking about wanting to see that *Stomp* production," he said sheepishly. "I saw in the paper that they are going to be performing at the Kauffman Center in Kansas City next weekend, and I thought you and the girls might like to have a night on the town."

Cora Mae was speechless. Since she was a little girl, she had always wanted to dance on stage, and seeing this production was just a huge coup for her. She had been in a few high school productions, but after that she didn't have the courage to pursue that childhood dream. Watching others, and knowing the training and dedication necessary to succeed, she appreciated large dance productions and loved the opportunity to go to productions when they came through.

"How did you get tickets, Eddie? This show has been sold out for weeks!"

"I have a friend who knows a guy who had tickets for sale. They're real good seats, too."

Tears welled up in Cora Mae's eyes as she threw her arms around his neck and gave him a kiss to stop time.

***

Cora Mae's eyes were still red and swollen when she left Eddie at the diner to continue phase two of her mission for Charlie Joe. She pulled on her mittens and wrapped her scarf around her neck as she walked down the street, thinking back on her late-night conversation with Charlie Joe a few weeks ago. It was like Charlie Joe to just show up on her doorstep in the middle of the night. That indelible wild heart of hers did not survive well in the confines of the four walls of her family's home. Since childhood, Charlie Joe had been known to wander the countryside at night. Her momma had fits about it, but no amount of spankings or groundings changed her spirit, and in the end, her papa had given in and allowed it. Charlie Joe had always respected her pappy's wishes and stayed clear of certain areas of the county that he deemed unsafe, and as a favor, neighbors and the local police were watchful of her whereabouts too. Her wanderings made her aware of all the animal traps in the county and even a few stills that were operating.

Charlie Joe had an uncanny ability to be in the right place at the right time, and more than once she had reported the whereabouts of stolen property or the abuse of an animal she happened upon. Most folks in the area gave Charlie Joe a respect beyond her years, and in return she was always truthful and direct in her dealings with them. The fact that her adoptive parents were black affected some folks who carried a heavy prejudice, and once when she was in high school, CJ had even taken the brunt of it in the form of a gang beating from a group of girls from the next county.

Jeremiah had been sick about it and had gotten the townsfolk together, black and white, to demonstrate in front of the courthouse while Charlie Joe was in the hospital. Cora Mae remembered that day very well, as it was the fall of their junior year, and Channel 7 News sent a crew to cover the story. Three days after the beating, the gang of girls was arrested and tried in court. Charlie Joe's life had never been an easy one, but Cora Mae had never heard her make excuses or complain about it. The fact that she came to her in the middle of the night to talk about Jeremiah carried some serious weight with Cora Mae.

Charlie Joe was worried that Jeremiah was giving up on her and would start seeing other girls. She admitted that she loved him, but somewhere inside she couldn't bring herself to marry him. CJ had worried her mind around the problem for days but admitting that she wanted to know about her birth-parents before she got married and had kids seemed like just an excuse to put him off. She had come to Cora Mae to see if her friend had any insight, thinking maybe she could offer some advice, seeing how she was removed from it and all.

Cora Mae couldn't provide any immediate insight, only offer moral support and comfort; but as she pondered it, she began to realize that all of CJ's life, she had struggled against racism. Oh, people who didn't know her adoptive parents liked her well enough, but CJ never brought her college friends home for Christmas and never accepted their invitations. Instead, she came back on Christmas break alone and spent her free time delivering holiday meals to the shut-ins.

One year Audrey Lemoine and Cora Mae had heard of a family whose three-year-old daughter had been admitted to the hospital for pneumonia. The father worked loading semitrailers for a local distribution center and due to a recession in the economy, had been temporarily laid off. Because of the drop in income, the family had to choose between not having Christmas and being able to afford health insurance. Audrey and Cora Mae had talked about the situation with Charlie Joe. The three formed a plan to buy gifts and surprise the family on Christmas Eve with a decorated tree and presents for the entire family. The delivery was anonymously made, with a single tag that simply read, "We Love You, Merry Christmas!"

Yes, Charlie Joe had known how to touch the lives of others. It was her own that she couldn't seem to figure out. Cora Mae suspected what needed to happen, and she was going to need help getting it done.

Walking into the sheriff's office, she stopped at the front desk where Jordan Morey, the Deputy Sheriff, sat.

"Morning, Jordan." She smiled as she greeted him. Looking about the office, she saw that Jeremiah's door was closed. It looked like someone was in the office with him, and it was a loud conversation they were having. "I need to talk with Jeremiah. Is this a bad time?"

"Cora Mae!" Jeremiah stepped out of his office. Mark Hubbard quietly stepped out behind him. "What are you doin' here? Haven't you heard?"

"Heard what?"

"Jordan. Take Cora Mae over to the hospital," Jeremiah ordered. "Cora Mae, I need you to take care of Audrey for me right now. Can you do that for me?"

The blood drained from Cora Mae's face as she took this information in. "What's going on, Jeremiah?"

"Neil's been shot. You need to go sit with Audrey and wait. She needs you right now."

23

Sweetwater, Missouri

Stuart Riedel was beside himself after he received the call from his son, Kevin. He tried calling Hank Lawson, the Deputy Sheriff, and when he couldn't reach him, he called Sheriff Langdon.

"We have another body out by the cemetery, Sheriff. I'm going to need help on this one. I have a trailer full of kids who have been instructed to leave the area immediately, but the killer could still be out there. It's a bad situation that could get a lot worse before the night is over."

"I'm on my way, Stuart. I'll call in help en route."

Stuart told Shirley as little as possible before leaving, but she knew it had been Kevin who had called.

"What's going on, Stuart?" she begged, trying not to sound hysterical. "Are the kids OK?"

"Kevin and Riley are together with the other kids. They are headed back into town now. They found another body while they were out on their hayride. The kids are pretty scared, but I think they are all OK for now." He pulled his gun out of the lockbox in the nightstand in their bedroom.

"Stuart." She worried as she watched him load the gun and holster it. He hadn't been able to handle a gun with his right hand since the injury and watching him now made her very afraid. She knew that his hand wasn't strong enough to handle the gun and using his left hand had never been a serious option. They came here, to a small town, so Stuart wouldn't have to be in these kinds of situations—the kinds where his life depended on his ability to shoot to kill.

He turned and stood in front of Shirley, his hand on her shoulders. He knew what was racing through her mind.

"I have to go do this, and I have to be able to protect those kids. I'm afraid I know the monster who's doing this, Shirley. I have backup coming. The sheriff is already on his way, and he's calling in reinforcements from Black Horse, Missouri as we speak. Lock the door behind me. I'll call you as soon as I know something," he promised as he kissed her good-bye. "I love you, Shirley." He turned and left the house.

She watched him as he got into their car and drove down the street. *Lord, protect him. Protect my children. Keep them safe,* she prayed as she turned the lock on the door and started for the kitchen. Knowing she wouldn't be able to sleep until she knew everyone was home and safe, she decided to heat some water and drink some tea. Filling the kettle and placing it on the stove, she heard their doorbell ring. She turned the heat off the stove and wiped her hands on a little tea towel that Riley had given her as a Mother's Day gift. She laid the towel down and walked to the door.

The frosted glass of the front door obscured the identity of the person waiting for her to answer. She wasn't expecting anyone. "Who is it?"

"Officer Danton, ma'am. I got a call from the sheriff to meet a Stuart Riedel at his home."

Shirley opened the door to a very tall man in a camel-colored overcoat. The stranger, who sported a goatee, looked like he had just had a haircut. Reaching into his pocket, he pulled out what looked like a badge, but it didn't look like the one that Stuart carried.

"My husband just left, Officer Danton," she told him.

"Are you alone then?" he asked as he stepped closer, placing his foot on the threshold.

***

The phone is what started it, Lance thought. *If she hadn't called, things might be different now.* Mombasa had just left when his phone rang. Riley's name came up on his screen, and Spade had confiscated his phone, checking his call logs. The questions started then. Of course, Spade knew all about Riley. He knew she had a twin brother and that her dad was working with Officer Hank Lawson as their new detective. What he hadn't known was that Lance had a thing for her.

Spade's physical size gave him a powerful presence, but it was the deadness of his eyes that frightened Lance the most.

"Tonight, we work together. You will do as I tell you."

Officer Hank Lawson was unconscious when Spade drove the nails through his hands and into the wooden fence that surrounded the cemetery. Lance had been instructed to hold Hank Lawson's body erect until the body was firmly nailed in place. The fact that he never gained consciousness was somehow comforting to Lance. It was more like nailing a rag doll down than a human being and made it less barbaric. The smell of gasoline clung to his clothes even now as he sat in the shadows, waiting.

Lance was not privy to what was about to happen. He was simply following orders, trying to stay alive. He was afraid that Hank Lawson's death was just a beginning. The officer had been in a financial bind, according to Spade, and had accepted an offer to watch the town for Mombasa. "Just be on call if I need you," he had been told, and he had been paid handsomely for this service. His fall from grace came in the form of a sin: not planting evidence on Meretrix's body that would point to Detective Riedel.

Sheriff Will Langdon was tough, keeping drugs out of the school and off the streets for the last few years. Two of Mombasa's men had been caught and arrested in Perry. Sheriff Langdon had a nose for the underground drug business and was relentless in his pursuit to keep it off his streets. His own grandson had been known to dabble in the drug business, but the sheriff was careful to keep close tabs on that past activity and keep it out of the public eye.

Officer Lawson's job was to scout the kids, find a weak link, and pass those names on to Mombasa. That's how Mombasa had found Lance. Meretrix was only a vessel to pull him into the inner circle. Being a courier over the last few months was simply a test. The expectations had changed for Lance, and tonight was his initiation.

Spade has been gone a long time, he thought as he checked his watch. The Hummer had been parked on a dark alley two streets over from Oliver Drive. Lance knew the area, as this was close to where Riley lived, but he didn't know the purpose of this errand. It had occurred to him that getting out and running might be a good idea, but he knew Spade would hunt him down. Any hope of ever getting out of this alive would be lost.

A dark figure approached the Hummer, and as the man slowly walked toward him, Lance could see him scrubbing his hands on what looked like a kitchen towel. He carried a small box under his arm and placed it on the floorboard under his feet before he climbed in behind the wheel of the vehicle. Closing his door, he punched in a phone number to Lance's cell phone and waited for an answer.

***

Sheriff Langdon stood in front of the burned corpse. The lights from the police car illuminated the body that still hung to the fire-charred wood. The pungent smell of burning flesh clung to his skin and hair as he used his flashlight to take a closer look at the remains. The medical examiner was on his way out. Seeing that Detective Stuart Riedel had just arrived on the scene, he clicked his flashlight off and walked to meet Stuart at the police car. Even from the road, Sheriff Langdon could smell the odor of the dead.

"The body was gutted. It looks like an accelerant was poured over it to maximize the burn. I'll have to take it back to the lab and run some tests before I can begin to identify the body. It might be a few days."

"I just got a call from Kevin. The kids are back at Janet Nelson's home and are waiting inside. They're pretty shaken up."

"I need to apologize to you, Stuart. I should have trusted you before now and given you free rein on this case. My grandson was involved in drugs at one point, and I've worked hard to help him start fresh again after he went through rehab. His mother moved them back here at the beginning of the school year. She is working as the new drama and music teacher in the high school. You might remember her, Helen Henry?"

"Yes, I remember her. She did a fantastic job with the winter program they just had."

"In any case, Stuart, I was wrong to limit your investigation. Maybe if I'd given you free rein before now, we wouldn't have another body on our hands."

"Where's Hank at, Sheriff?"

"I haven't been able to reach him all day. These last couple of weeks, I've been wondering why I keep him, to be honest. This is the second time he's gone off radar when I needed him. He's good with people but hasn't been very reliable as of late."

The medical examiner pulled up behind the sheriff's car, and he and his small crew began unloading equipment.

"I'd better start taking pictures, then head over to the Nelson's to start interviewing the kids. Any chance you can call in some help on this one, Sheriff?"

"I'll call the Blackhorse Police Department. Jeremiah Stone is the sheriff over there. Maybe he can send over a couple of officers and hopefully come over himself as well. He's a good man."

***

Blackhorse, Missouri

Jeremiah's desk rang. Anger etched across his face as he picked up the receiver and listened. It was the Sweetwater Police Department. Sheriff Will Langdon was asking for help. A group of teenagers had happened upon another body. Facts started lining up in Jeremiah's head: two recent murders in a town only a few miles over, Neil Lemoine is shot by his estranged brother, Shaun and Charlie Joe is missing and presumed hostage. *I know where you are, Charlie Joe. I'm going to get you somewhere safe and make sure Shaun pays for this. This and whatever else he's done.* "I'm on my way, Sheriff. I'll be there in twenty minutes."

Mark Hubbard stood, listening to Jeremiah. "Didn't you hear me? I said Shaun took Charlie Joe."

"I heard you, Mark," he said as he rounded the desk and grabbed his coat from the back of the chair. "I need you to call Moses."

Mark Hubbard, a professional animal tracker and Moses Aikins were best friends. He understood what Jeremiah was asking when he said to call Moses. Moses' family lived in the woods around the lake. He knew every cabin, every cabin owner, and all the happenings around the lake within a twenty-mile radius. Those woods were his home. "You think he hid her in his pappy's cabin?"

"I think Shaun has been busy in these parts for a bit. Likely he's been using that cabin for a home base while he's been here. Take Moses and find her. Shaun won't be there right now, so we have some time to get her out before he returns, but you have to hurry, Mark."

"Yes, Sir. Do you want me to call you when we find her?"

"Call the dispatch when you find her. I won't have cell service where I'm going." Jeremiah stopped at the dispatch desk and placed a call out to his two deputies. He needed them to head over to Sweetwater and help with the investigation. Mark and Moses would take over finding Charlie Joe.

24

Sweetwater, Missouri

Kevin and Dylan had driven the tractor-trailer back to the Nelson's as fast as they could while still keeping everyone safe. The group was unusually quiet until the front door was locked and everyone was inside. Janet's parents were home and immediately were informed about the burning corpse found at the cemetery. They placed another call to the sheriff and were assured that an officer would be there shortly. Mrs. Nelson offered refreshments, but no one accepted her offer of comfort. Gathering in small groups about the room, they sought the comfort of one another's presence in stunned silence.

Kevin felt chilly despite the warmth of the room. His coat was buttoned up the front. He started to remove his gloves when Riley's cell phone vibrated in his pocket. Riley was standing across the room from him with Janet and Amy, her two closest friends. Watching her, he reached for the phone and saw that Lance's name was on the screen. He flipped the phone open to answer the call but didn't say anything.

"Your mother was a beautiful woman. She wanted me to tell you she loved you," the deep voice breathed, waiting for a reaction. Kevin stood stone-still and silent, his eyes boring into Riley. Feeling his eyes on her, she turned around and saw Kevin's pale countenance. "I have a package for your father. Tell him to pick it up at One-Two-One-One Riverdale Road in one hour. And make sure he comes alone."

"Something's wrong," Riley said to no one in particular as she left her friends and crossed the room to Kevin.

The caller had hung up without waiting for a response. Kevin immediately called home, ignoring Riley's presence next to him. The phone rang and rang. No response. He called his dad's cell phone.

"Hello?" Stuart said as he unpacked his camera from the trunk of his car.

"Dad!" Kevin yelled. "He called again. He's seen Mom!"

"Whoa! Calm down! What do you mean he called again?"

Riley stood next to him, intensely listening as Kevin recounted the first call, then the call he just received.

"Stay where you are, Kevin, and keep Riley safe," Stuart instructed, dropping the camera back into the trunk and heading toward the sheriff's police car.

"What about Mom and Rachelle?" Kevin asked, his adrenaline kicking in as his mind raced over the horrible possibilities.

"Just sit tight." Stuart snapped the phone shut, ending the call.

***

Sheriff Will Langdon was on his radio in the police car when Stuart came up behind him. Sheriff Jeremiah Stone had arrived a few minutes earlier and was standing at the car door next to Sheriff Langdon. "Will, I have reason to believe that my family has become a target."

Sheriff Will Langdon ended his radio transmission and turned to him. "What's going on, Stuart?"

"My son has received two calls tonight, both on my daughter's cell phone. I don't know how this person got the number, but Kevin tells me he called the first time just before they came upon the body here. The second call came in just now and made a direct reference to my wife at home, with a demand that I be at One-Two-One-One Riverdale Road in one hour. I need someone to take over here so I can go home and make sure she's OK." Detective Riedel's outward calmness was very deceiving. Inwardly, professional training waged war with his protective instinct.

Two Black Horse police cruisers pulled up behind the medical examiner's vehicle on the side of the road and approached them.

"You're not going alone, Stuart," the Sheriff Langdon ordered. "Jeremiah, this is Detective Stuart Riedel. Stuart, this is Sheriff Jeremiah Stone from Blackhorse, Missouri."

"Pleasure to meet you, Detective Riedel. I wish the circumstances were different," he said as he offered a handshake. "I'd be happy to take you back to your house if you wouldn't mind my company. Sheriff Langdon can stay here with my other two officers and work the crime scene while we check out your house."

"Thank you." Stuart was relieved to have a fellow officer go with him. Although Sheriff Stone wasn't an overly large man, he had a strong and commanding presence. Stuart's strongest gift was the gift of discernment. He was able to accurately read a person's character very quickly and what he saw in Sheriff Stone gave him great comfort. Protective instinct was winning the inward war with professionalism as he turned to make his way to the police cruiser.

"I'll have my radio on me at all times," Sheriff Langdon stated. "I want a radio report of your findings as soon as you can. In the meantime I'm heading over to the Nelson's to see if those kids can give me any insight into what's going on. Let's move."

Stuart Riedel was already advancing on his police cruiser when Sheriff Jeremiah Stone called for him. "Riedel! We take my car." Sheriff Stone strode towards the Blackhorse patrol car and got in the front seat. Detective Riedel opened the door and climbed in the passenger's side.

"Before we head over to your house, detective, I want to make a few things clear. First, you will stay in the car until I have swept the house. I don't know all the details of what is going on right now, but from what I do know, it appears that you are a target. I won't have you shot on my watch. Understand?"

Stuart Riedel looked at his new colleague. All he could do was nod in agreement.

"Secondly, I need to know how you plan to protect yourself if things go bad. Sheriff Langdon filled me in on your injury to your right hand. Can you shoot a gun?"

"I've been doing physical therapy and am getting stronger with my right hand. I can shoot a gun just fine." Pride, fear and anxiety mixed into the response Stuart gave. He had been doing physical therapy, but he hadn't tried shooting a gun with his right hand yet. He could shoot with his left hand, but accuracy was sacrificed when he did. He really didn't have time to discuss this right now. They needed to get moving.

Sheriff Stone smiled at Stuart as he started the car and turned to reach into the back seat as he spoke. "You look like a man who can hold his own, but just in case, I have a light weight cross-bow that I carry everywhere with me. It's lighter than a traditional handgun and is more sensitive on the trigger. You don't have to squeeze as hard to get a shot off."

He handed the cross bow to Stuart before putting the car in gear and turning onto the pavement. "Treat it like a rifle and in low wind situations like this evening, you'll hit your mark every time."

Stuart was overwhelmed. In an instant, this man had identified his greatest weakness. Instead of thinking less of him as a police officer and as a man, Sheriff Stone had given him two gifts: encouragement and hope. Although he'd never used a crossbow before, he was confident that he could stand on his own if it came to it.

"One more thing, Stuart. Can I call you that?"

"Sure."

"I think I know who the killer is. I don't know why he's killing, but I have a suspicion."

"Tell me what you know."

***

Kevin was shaking. There were so many emotions bottled up inside, with fear and anger being the strongest at the moment. He wasn't given to just sitting by when someone he loved could be in danger, and although he knew he should stay and make sure Riley remained safe, he couldn't suppress the urge to leave for home. *I am closer than Dad is and can get there sooner,* he thought. He turned to Riley as he pulled his phone out of his pocket, keeping hers with him.

"I want you to keep this in case Mom or Dad call, Riley. I'm going to run by the house and make sure Mom is OK. You stay here. Don't leave, you understand?"

Riley didn't respond to Kevin other than to take the phone he offered and nod agreement. The thought of anything happening to either Mom or Rachelle was unfathomable. She couldn't wrap her mind around it and didn't understand the import of what he was telling her until he quietly slipped from the room. Standing there, alone in a crowded room, it began to hit her what he had said. He was going home. She looked down at the phone he gave her and realized it was not hers. *The person responsible for the burning corpse had called Kevin,* she thought. *Kevin is going after him!*

Looking around the room, she saw Amy and Janet softly talking together. No one in the room appeared to notice that Kevin had left. Pocketing Kevin's phone, she made her way over to Amy and Janet.

"I'm going to use the bathroom in the back bedroom, if that is OK, Janet," she said.

"Sure," Janet said. "Dad said the sheriff called and is on his way over here now to interview everyone. I expect he'll be here fairly soon."

Riley gave her a half smile and nodded understanding before turning toward the back of the house. The bedroom at the back of the house had a sliding glass door that led out onto the deck of the swimming pool. Riley planned to use that door to make a quiet retreat and walk the fifteen blocks back to her house. The temperatures were dropping outside, but she had a warm coat on and knew the back streets well enough that she was confident she could make it home in about thirty minutes. It would be too much of a risk to ask for a ride, and she didn't want anyone keeping her from her family when they were in need. She paused at the closet door right outside the bedroom and looked behind her. No one was watching as she gently opened the closet door, reached inside and slipped the gun into her coat pocket before heading on back to the bedroom.

25

Charlie Joe had no idea how long she had been unconscious. Her head was pounding and her hands were numb from the bindings. Her whole body ached from the cold, but she was still alive. *Shaun will be back soon*, she thought. *He was serious about hunting me. I've got to find a way out of here—a way out of this situation.* She tested the bindings on her hands again, but they were tight and unforgiving. The temperature had dropped outside, and the moon was rising in the east casting a soft glow through a small window of the cabin cellar. *Shaun had told Neil he would bring me to their hunting cabin.* Looking around she could see old jars of peaches lining the wooden shelves. Onions and potatoes lay spread out on a makeshift table with sawhorses as legs. The sound of slow dripping water could be heard in the shadows and contributed to the musty smell that permeated the cellar.

Pulling herself upright, she found that she could bite the ropes around her wrists and loosen them a bit. There wasn't a lot of give, but if she worked it right, she might be able to slip a hand out. After a few minutes of gnawing, she gave up and looked around her again. The board she was tied to ran along the wall under the shelving where the peaches were lined up. She pulled herself fully upright and tried to stand. The cellar ceiling was low and with her hands tied, she wasn't able to stand full upright. She still had her boots on. Using the beam to steady herself, she reached her left foot towards a jar of peaches and tried to inch it towards her. The weight of her leg tilted the whole shelf forwards and several jars slid to the edge before she dropped her foot back to the floor. She didn't want the whole thing crashing down, just one jar. She tried again and this time, with the jar already at the edge, she was able to inch it towards her so that it fell and broke just a few feet from her. Unfortunately, the jar didn't shatter as she hoped. Instead, a small jagged piece broke off from the bottom and the contents of the jar spilled out. The jagged piece was just out of reach of her boot, but the jar itself was within reach and she was able to roll it closer to her.

Now the problem was how to get the jar up to her hands where she could use the edge to cut the rope. CJ put her right boot heel on her left toe and slipped the boot downward, off her foot. She slipped her sock off and grabbed the jar with her toes, lifting it up to her hands. The edge of the jar cut the tender skin on the underside of her foot and blood trickled down onto the floor. *That's going to hurt when I have to run, but that's the least of my worries right now.*

She could hear an owl hooting outside. This was a good sign. When man walked through the woods, nature became quiet. It meant she was still alone and still had a chance to get away—at least for the moment.

***

Sweetwater, Missouri

Stuart sat beside Sheriff Jeremiah Stone, waiting for him to tell him what he knew. Sheriff Stone wasn't quick to relay information and this angered Stuart somewhat. He wasn't used to the slow, thoughtful response of Midwest people. He had to check himself. *Just because people talked slow, responded slow, didn't mean they weren't smart.*

"I grew up in Blackhorse, Detective. I know the people here. I know their history," Jeremiah began. "Two boys grew up in an abusive home—and by abusive, I mean it was as bad as it can get. One boy turned out to be a pretty upstanding man, for the most part. The other, well, he took after his pappy. No one really understands how one boy could turn out okay while the other didn't, but there it is."

"So you think a boy who grew up in an abusive home came home to kill? That doesn't make sense."

"What I'm trying to tell you is that this particular boy learned how to kill from his pappy. Like I said, it was an abusive home. No one knows for sure what really happened behind those closed walls, but most people here believe the two boys were made to watch as their pappy murdered their momma. It was a right of passage, so to speak, in a very demented mind."

"He was training them to kill?"

"In a very real sense of the word. Nothing could be proved, but it wasn't long after their momma's funeral that their pappy died mysteriously. He was a drunk, but he knew the land and how to survive on it. A man like that doesn't walk out into a winter storm and break his neck in a ravine. Even stone drunk, the ol' man knew better."

"So you believe this boy killed his father."

Jeremiah looked over at Stuart as he drove. He didn't justify that question with a response. "His name is Shaun and he left the area a few days after his pappy was found. His brother, Neil, stayed and took over the family business. Neil settled down. Married. Had a couple of kids. He's a good man. His brother Shaun, though—he's another story."

"Why would he come back here, though? What's the catch?"

"A man like Shaun is driven by two things: a desire to kill and acceptance. Monetary rewards are secondary, although a necessary evil in order to survive. Somewhere along the way, Shaun perfected his killing. He got creative. He's always been a highly intelligent person and it fits a serial killer's profile. What I don't understand is why you would be a target—or why Charlie Joe has been taken hostage by him."

"What? I don't know anything about a hostage."

"Shaun shot his brother earlier in an altercation. Charlie Joe was at the scene when it happened and he took her when he left." Jeremiah had pulled up to the curb in front of Stuart's house and put the Blackhorse police cruiser in park. "Remember what you promised me, Stuart. You will wait here while I sweep the house."

Stuart didn't answer as he stared at the front porch. The light was off. Shirley always left the light on when someone was gone. The weight of what he feared Jeremiah might find hung heavy in the air. Shirley had not answered the phone when Stuart tried to call her, but if she were in the shower, she would not have heard the phone ring. Having a moment of renewed hope, he dialed the number again.

"The caller told Kevin that he had a package for me at One-Two-One-One Riverdale Road," Stuart said as he waited for Shirley to answer the phone.

Sheriff Jeremiah Stone sat quietly, watching Stuart. Waiting.

Stuart nodded, unable to take his eyes off the home they had moved into just a few months ago. *All* the lights are off. Why did Shirley turn off all the lights? *My greatest fear is being realized*, he thought, struggling to keep his composure and focus. *If I lose it now, I won't do anyone any good. I have to keep it together.*

"You have ten minutes, Jeremiah."

Sheriff Stone got out and quickly approached the house, gun drawn. He stopped at the front door and pulled on a pair of latex gloves so as to not leave any prints inside the house.

Stuart watched him as he pushed open the front door, gun low and ready, and disappeared inside. He checked his watch and noted the time. He had done similar house searches many times over the years, and in his mind, he imagined the route Jeremiah was taking, searching each room before moving to the next, ever vigilant that the perpetrator could still be present in the home. He would move from the front foyer down the hall, checking closets and around corners, securing, then moving forward. Once the ground floor had been covered, he would move up the staircase to the bedrooms, methodically searching and securing, until all the rooms had been checked.

Two minutes. *Think, Stuart. If it really was this Shaun person that Jeremiah believes it to be, why would he do this? Why murder a girl from Kansas City, then come back to town and murder again? Maybe the person at the cemetery was another body from the KC area, and Sweetwater had just become the site of execution. It wasn't too far off I-70, but there were some two-lane roads you had to travel to get to there. Not exactly an ideal location for a dumping ground because of the lack of exit routes until you reached the interstate again. But why call into Riley's cell phone? Why did Kevin have Riley's phone? Maybe she dropped it, and Kevin was holding it for her when the call came through,* he thought. *How is Riley connected to the killer? Why am I being targeted? Is the sheriff somehow involved? And where the hell is Hank?*

Eight minutes. Still no lights on in the house. It was a big house, and a thorough, methodical search could take the full ten minutes, but he doubted it. Stuart got out of the car and closed the door. He pulled the crossbow from the front seat, loading it with a metal arrow from the quiver before starting for the front door. Jeremiah stepped out onto the porch before Stuart reached the front steps. He had his radio in his hand, and his gun was holstered. He held up his left hand as if to stop Stuart from coming any closer as he called in to Sheriff Langdon.

"Sheriff Stone to Sheriff Langdon."

"Go ahead, Jeremiah."

"We have a crime scene. I need the team to come here next." Jeremiah watched Stuart closely as he relayed as little information as possible.

Stuart's face went pale, and his ears started ringing. He couldn't focus, but felt his whole body go tense. Charging forward, he tried to push past Jeremiah to get into the house. Jeremiah bear hugged him and took him to the ground, handcuffing his wrists behind his back to prevent him from going in and having to live with what he would find for the rest of his life.

"I'm going to need some backup here, Sheriff," Jeremiah panted into the radio. "Your detective is out of service, and we have a killer on the loose, with another threat to expire in less than an hour on Riverdale Road. What are your orders?"

"I called FBI already, Sheriff Stone. Sheriff Langdon is in route to your location now." Doris Hall, the county dispatcher, sounded on the channel. She had been at her station for hours monitoring the radio frequencies for the county. Because she knew that officers from another jurisdiction had been summoned into her area, she followed strict police radio protocol and kept all radio communication to fifteen seconds or less. "Is Detective Riedel with you? I need to talk to him. Break."

"He's indisposed at the moment. Go ahead," Sheriff Stone said, being used to the call and echo of police dispatch protocol.

"Matthew Johnson, the US marshal from Chicago, called in looking for Detective Riedel. He had a message he wanted passed on immediately. Break."

"Go ahead," said Sheriff Stone, not sure if Stuart was listening or not.

"The bullet ballistics had a hit in their archives. A man by the name of Lamar Carver. Goes by Mombasa in the underground. Break."

"Go ahead."

"Hit man by the name of Spade works for him. No identifying information available. Break."

"Go ahead." Sheriff Jeremiah Stone looked up to see Sheriff Langdon pull up to the curb and get out of the car.

"Last seen two days ago in Wichita. Highly dangerous. Use extreme caution. Advise FBI assistance to apprehend. Break."

Stuart lay on the ground, subdued into numbness. His mind was blank as he tried to focus on the approaching feet across the lawn. Drawing into himself, he prayed. *Lord, Shirley is in your hands. I wasn't there for her. Mombasa and Spade are attacking my family, and I have no control. No matter what happens tonight, whatever happens, it's out of my hands, but never out of your control. Nothing ever surprises you. You are all knowing. Help me, Lord. I feel so small, so weak.*

Sheriff Langdon diverted back to the new crime scene instead of interviewing the kids at the Nelson residence. An ambulance arrived a few minutes after Sheriff Langdon screeched to a stop and parked at the curb. Another black and tan had arrived with lights flashing. People were talking, but Stuart couldn't understand what they were saying. *Rachelle. Where's Rachelle?* He mumbled as his mind began to clear, and he began to regain control of his senses. A sense of calm overcame him, and he relaxed, knowing that God knew how things were going to unfold. God was in control, and all Stuart needed to do was trust and go forward. He couldn't deny fear, but he could keep it from dominating him.

26

Sweetwater, Missouri

The blue '68 Mustang rolled to a stop behind the ambulance that had just arrived. Neighbors began to stand on their porches, trying to catch a glimpse of the goings-on at the Riedel home. Most knew that Stuart was involved with law enforcement but didn't understand or didn't ask what it was exactly that he did. Kevin got out of his car and strode toward the house. Sheriff Langdon saw Kevin and intercepted him on the lawn.

"Hold on, Kevin. Where are you going, son?"

"None of your damn business," he growled. "Get out of my way."

The sheriff was quite a bit larger than Kevin and made his presence known by standing face-to-face with Kevin. "Look at me, Kevin." Waiting for the young man to turn his eyes and face him, he took a deep breath and proceeded with blunt honesty. "Your mom is dead, and your sister is missing. We don't know who we are dealing with, but from the two calls you received tonight, it looks like your family is a major target. I need you to pull it together and tell me exactly what you know."

Kevin realized his dad was on the ground with handcuffs on. Pushing the sheriff aside, he jogged to his dad and knelt down.

"Dad, are you OK?"

Sheriff Jeremiah Stone stood next to Stuart. Seeing Kevin, he knelt down beside them. "Stuart, if I release you, will you promise to not try to go into the house?"

Stuart looked at Kevin and saw the shock that he felt reflecting back from him. "I promise. You can release me now."

Once the handcuffs were removed, he stood up and dusted the dried, broken leaves from his clothes. Sheriff Langdon joined the solemn group as uniformed officers worked the crime scene inside.

Two FBI agents had just arrived and were directed toward the sheriff. Showing their badges, they introduced themselves. Stuart recognized Special Agent Brad Engel. Special Agent Kent Dime was new to the force.

"What do we have here?" Agent Engel asked, directing the question to Sheriff Langdon.

Kevin took the phone out of his pocket and handed it to Agent Engel. "I received two calls tonight on my sister's phone. Lance Meton's name came up on the screen both times, but it wasn't him calling. It was an older man with a very deep voice. The first call came when we were still out on the hayride, before we came up on the burning body."

Both officers had been given an updated report on the night's events prior to arriving on scene at the Riedel home. The first body was already en route to the state medical examiner so an identification could be made as soon as possible.

Kevin's attention was drawn to the three EMTs as they lifted the body-heavy gurney down the steps and toward the ambulance. His mind went blank. Sheriff Jeremiah Stone placed a heavy hand on Kevin's shoulder, effectively drawing his mind back to the question Agent Engel had asked.

"Kevin, did you hear me?" Engel gently prodded.

Kevin's eyes focused back on the group, and he looked around at each individual. "The first call. He just said, 'You're next,' then hung up. The second call came after we had arrived at the Nelsons' house. If you look at the call log on the phone, it came in less than twenty minutes ago. All he said the second time was something about my mom saying she loved me. I don't remember exactly," he admitted, looking down.

Stuart could see that Kevin's initial anger was giving way to a deep sadness, but the night wasn't over yet, and the killer was setting another trap.

"You called me right after the second phone call, Kevin. He made a reference to your mom, then told you he had a package for me. I was to meet him at One-Two-One-One Riverdale Road in one hour. Is that right?"

"Yes. That's it. That's what he said."

"Why would the caller contact you, Kevin? What's the connection?"

"He wasn't calling me. He was calling Riley, my twin sister. It's her phone. The number that pops up is Lance's. That's a guy she made friends with from school. I told her not to see him anymore, but like I said, it wasn't his voice on the phone."

"That address is an abandoned house not far from where the first body was found a few weeks ago," Stuart said. "I had forensics do a ballistics test on the bullet casing. It came back as a signature for a man by the name of Lamar Carver. He is a drug lord out of Kansas City who employs a man only known to us as Spade. We have very little information on Spade other than he is extremely dangerous. My youngest daughter is missing, and we have forty minutes to devise a plan and set it in motion, people. Help me. What ideas do you have?"

"So we have another potential missing person," Engel said, recapping what they knew up to this point. "Your youngest daughter and this Lance person. We have two dead bodies and instructions to be at an address determined by the caller."

Agent Dime came forward. "Tell us about the rendezvous point."

"I have a county map in my car. Follow me." Sheriff Langdon turned back toward the street. He had unintentionally parked under a streetlamp, making it easy to view the map and decide a course of action. Pulling the map from his glove compartment and spreading it open across the hood of the car, he pointed to the location identified by the caller. "The old wooden farmhouse sits on an S-curve. A hedgerow runs along the county road north of the house, with a deep ravine south. West of the house is an open field of about ten acres of pasture, with a thick line of timber. There are no lights and four points of entry, with dense undergrowth on three sides. It's an extremely dangerous position to try to place officers in to cover Stuart. Anyone have any ideas?"

Special Agent Engel looked at his partner. "How many officers do you have available?"

"You're looking at them right here, unless you use the men inside who are working the crime scene. I can't locate my deputy sheriff, Hank Lawson. He's been missing all day."

Agent Dime looked around the group. "Was there anything on the burned corpse to make you suspect it was your missing officer, Sheriff?"

The sheriff was stunned. It had never occurred to him that Hank could be dead. In fact, he hadn't believed it could be anyone from his town, or anyone he might know.

"The first body was a young woman from KC. What makes you think tonight's body could be my missing officer?"

"Has he ever just gone missing like that before?"

Sheriff Langdon didn't have an immediate answer, and the pause he gave prompted Agent Engel to head into the house and make sure none of the available officers left the scene. They would need every available badge to have any hope of pulling this off successfully.

***

Riley had quietly left the Nelson home by slipping out the patio door off the main bedroom at the back of the house. Staying to the shadows, she had made her way across town to the edge of Oliver Drive, where she crouched beside two trash barrels left out near the street. She could see the chaos at the front of her house. She watched as three EMTs loaded a body into the ambulance and drove off, leaving a gap in the cars that lined the edge of Oliver Drive. Most of the neighbors had been driven back inside by the cold night air, but a few still lingered at the edges of their respective lawns, listening and watching for evidence of what had happened in their neighborhood.

She spotted Kevin and her dad under the streetlamp with a group of law enforcement officers. Another officer she didn't recognize was in the group, along with Sheriff Langdon. Jackets embossed with huge

FBI letters were worn by two of the men in the group, easily identifying them from the others. She didn't know how many people were still in the house, but several had already left by the front door and were waiting on the lawn. She had forgotten her gloves at Janet's house and stuck her fingers in her mouth to warm them up. Pulling her hat further down over her ears and crouching back into the shadows a little more, she watched as the coroner's car drove by her. She heard a rattling can being blown down the alley behind her as a wind gust blew through. A piece of plastic caught on the wire fence beat back and forth. Typical night noises surrounded her as she thought about what to do next.

Backing down the alley, being careful not to be seen, she kept close to the middle of the alley. Many people kept their trashcans along this alley and hitting one would create enough noise to cause attention. She had not seen Rachelle on the front lawn. She had stood and watched as EMTs removed one body bag from the home—at least, only one that she saw—there was a good chance that both her mom and Rachelle were okay, hidden somewhere in the house—that the body bag held someone she didn't know. Her stomach ached and she felt nauseated. She tried to keep calm, but the stress was overwhelming. She felt dizzy and placed her hand on the fence rail in front of her to steady herself. Her mom couldn't be dead. It had to be someone else in the home. Kevin had said the caller had a package for her dad. Worried about how best to help, she stopped to think.

"Riley." A voice came from just feet in front of her.

Startled, she froze. She recognized the voice as a hand came from behind her and smothered her screams. Everything went black.

27

Sweetwater, Missouri

The driveway to the abandoned house on 1211 Riverdale Road was a good five hundred feet long and had deep ruts that prevented Stuart from driving farther than just the length of his car before he had to stop. He could see the dark shadowed line of the hedgerow to the north and the timberline that hid a deep ravine to the south. There were no lights on in the old house, but the sky was clear, and a full moon was high in the night sky, casting an eerie light around him. He sat in the car, waiting. He still had five minutes before the deadline to be here, and he wanted to give the police time to create a perimeter around the house before he walked in.

Stepping out of the car and into the freezing night air, Stuart checked the weight of his gun in his left hand. His right hand still wasn't strong enough to hold the gun, and although he had practiced from time to time out at the shooting range, he was a poor shot with his left hand. *Lord, I can't do this alone,* he prayed, standing there in the darkness. Knowing that the presence of the gun would only endanger everyone, he put it on the front seat of his car and closed the door. He would go in unarmed. Although the crossbow that Sheriff Stone had given him was an excellent weapon, it was too large to conceal.

Putting his hands in his pockets, because he didn't know what else to do with them, he slowly began the walk up the driveway toward the house. As he did so, he felt the cold metal of Riley's phone in his pocket. Special Agent Engel had given him Riley's phone in case the caller tried to make contact again.

***

From the timberline they watched the house and waited. Uniformed men had accessed the rendezvous point from various sites, leaving the main entrance for Detective Riedel to use. Spade looked through a night scope with a silencer. "I'm counting twelve officers around the house."

Riley was bound and gagged, lying on the floor in the backseat of the Hummer. Lance didn't know what Spade had used on her to make her go unconscious so quickly. Her breathing had been very shallow when they left her to make their way through the field to the timberline, and he was worried she might already be dead. He could compartmentalize one killing. The death of Hank Lawson was difficult, but because he was unconscious when Spade gutted him and set his body aflame, Lance was convinced he didn't feel anything.

He didn't know what errand Spade had completed when he left Lance in the Hummer back in town, and he wasn't sure what was in the box that was left on the steps of the old house. It was heavy, whatever it was, and it slid around inside the box. The longer Lance had held it, the more it began to smell. Surely Spade would let Riley go. He was just using her to scare him. He could be tough and show Spade that he could handle this, but he would tell him that Riley had to be released. They could leave her bound on the side of the road, if necessary. *Someone would see her and stop to help* he rationalized as he watched Spade put a different piece on the rifle he carried into the timber.

***

Without speaking, Spade opened the canvas pack he brought and handed Lance a pair of night-vision goggles. He put his rifle down and noiselessly showed him how to position them on his face so he could watch and learn. *The boy was proving to have some mettle after all,* he thought. The night was still young, though, and there was a lot of information that had yet to be disclosed to the boy. For now the plan was unfolding nicely. The girl was an unexpected gift, and seeing how pretty she was, he could understand the leanings of a young man. In this business, though, it wasn't safe to have ties. Invariably, they became a weak link that had to be eliminated, or they would surely cause your capture and arrest. Explaining this to Lance would be a waste of time. Better for him to see and experience death, to get a taste for it. So far he appeared to be detached from these townspeople, and if he had developed any sentimental attachments, they didn't appear to carry much weight with the boy. He appeared to be unconcerned about the girl, but again, he may not fully realize what was happening.

Refocusing on the task at hand, they turned back to watch the scene unfold. Sure that Lance was alert and attentive, he raised the rifle and secured the silencer, sighting in his prey.

***

Kevin had been instructed to stay behind, and for safety reasons, he was told to return to the Nelsons' house. The sheriff ordered Officer Hayes to follow him over in his patrol car to make sure that both he and Riley were safe and accounted for.

After watching Kevin park in the street and making sure that he saw brake lights flash off and his car door open, Sheriff Jeremiah Stone stepped out of the patrol car to follow Kevin into the house on Tenth Street. He did a quick scan of the street and surrounding houses, looking for anything abnormal or out of the ordinary as he escorted him to the front door. Lights showed through the front windows, but no one could be seen inside the house. Mr. Nelson opened the heavy wooden door of the house to meet them on the small cement porch of the home. His hair was disheveled, and his face was a bit pale from the stress of the evening.

"Evening, Sheriff," he greeted him as he turned his attention to Kevin. "Did you find her?"

Kevin's radar was on high alert. Riley was still at the Nelson's when he slipped out of the room, and with such a crowd of close friends surrounding her, he was sure she would not leave. It never occurred to him that she might try to follow him. Hope sprang up, and for a moment, he thought it might not be Riley Mr. Nelson was referring to.

"Who's missing, Mr. Nelson?"

"Riley is, Kevin. No one has seen her for at least an hour. We've checked the whole house, and I've personally walked the perimeter of my property looking for her. We called the police fifteen minutes ago. I thought your car pulling up was the result of that call."

Pushing past Mr. Nelson, Kevin entered the room and quickly scanned for Janet. Seeing her in the kitchen, he approached her, trying to control his anger.

"Where did Riley go, Janet? I know she wouldn't have left without talking to you first," he accused.

Janet's eyes were red and swollen as she turned and met his burning anger. She knew that he blamed her, and the only thing she could offer him was truth. Riley had taught her a thing or two about honesty, even when others weren't looking. If something happened to her friend, she would never forgive herself. Riley was like a sister to her.

"She saw you take a phone call, Kevin. She saw that you were upset," she fired back at him, meeting his anger with a measure of her own guilt. "Riley asked me if she could use the bathroom in the master bedroom. I thought she needed some time to gather herself together, so I didn't check on her right away. When I did go back to see if she was all right, she was gone. The sliding glass door to the pool was slightly open. As soon as I found it, I knew she had left and told my dad."

Sheriff Jeremiah Stone and Mr. Nelson had joined Kevin in the kitchen, catching the end of Janet's explanation. Turning to his radio, Sheriff Stone tried to reach Sheriff Langdon to let him know, but each attempt was met with dead air space.

"I'm going to go out to the car and see if I can call up the sheriff in the cruiser. You stay put, Kevin. You understand?" he ordered, making eye contact with Mr. Nelson before leaving the room.

The police cruiser sat in apparent quiet on the street, but inside the radio was humming with activity. He could hear the sheriff giving position orders. Knowing that a takedown was in progress, he didn't want to signal on a channel that was obviously tagged for essential radio traffic. Kevin's sister was missing, and she was now his primary concern. Getting back out of the cruiser, he made his way back to the house to begin interviewing people. Maybe someone knew something, some little bit of information that might clue him in to Riley's target destination.

Stepping back into the warmth of the house, he could hear an argument growing intense.

"I'm not letting go of you, Kevin, until you calm down." Dylan held Kevin pinned to the floor in an obvious wrestling position. Dylan outweighed Kevin by a good fifteen pounds, but Kevin's emotions were running high, and the adrenaline rush was giving him an advantage. Dylan was struggling to keep him down.

Mr. Nelson stood back a few feet from the boys on the floor, holding a small, bloodied towel to his face. Sheriff Stone took stock of the situation and knelt down on the floor next to Kevin's head. "I need your help, Kevin. Can you pull yourself together and help me find your sister?"

Relaxing against Dylan, Kevin looked up at the officer. His dad had been a part of law enforcement his whole life. Every close friend his dad had was an officer in some capacity, and bred a trust that was not questioned.

"I have to find her," Kevin said. "I think I know where she might be, but I'm not sharing that information unless you promise to take me with you."

Sheriff Stone scanned the crowd, his eyes resting on the young man who held Kevin pinned to the floor. Nodding to Dylan, he silently agreed to Kevin's request.

Dylan released his hold and helped Kevin up off the floor.

Kevin and Sheriff Stone stood face-to-face, man-to-man. "You'll tell me what you know, and I'll tell you what to do," he said with calm authority. "You give the slightest indication that you aren't going to obey my orders, and you'll find your ass in the backseat of my cruiser in handcuffs."

Kevin wasn't going to risk the chance. Boundaries were expected, but they could be tested, and if he had an opportunity to ensure Riley was safe and OK, he wasn't about to waste it.

"Deal."

28

Sweetwater, Missouri

Riley felt the rough carpet against her face, but when she opened her eyes, she could see nothing but darkness. The odor of new carpet and the very cramped space told her she was facedown on the floor of a vehicle. She tried to turn over but could only manage to turn her shoulders enough to see the window above her feet. Something heavy was covering her, pressing her into the floor, and the weight of it on her back made her arms ache underneath her. She tried to push up again, but she was bound too tight to maneuver very much. Riley took a deep breath to calm herself. Thinking back over what had happened, she remembered the voice. *Lance. What was he doing in the alley behind my house? Who grabbed me from behind? Was Lance the one who set that person on fire?* Her hands were bound, but her mind was racing over the questions that had been building up inside since they first came upon the fire.

Lord, please help me. Lance is in trouble. I know that deep down he's a good person, and whatever he's been drawn into, he can decide to get out of, but not without your help. I'm bound here and scared, but I know you will protect me. Protect us both, and please keep my family safe, she prayed. Whatever drug they used on her was strong. She felt herself losing consciousness again and fought against it. Riley drew a sense of calm from speaking with God, and her faith gave her courage. Whatever happened, whatever she had to face, she wouldn't have to face it alone, she thought as her mind succumbed to darkness again.

***

The driveway to the abandoned farmhouse opened into a grassy knoll with a mature walnut tree at the top of it. Behind the tree, Stuart could see the outline of the house in the moonlight. The upstairs window had been broken out, and the front door hung on a rusty hinge that creaked as the night breeze played back and forth with the door. Stuart knew that Sheriff Langdon's deputies were close and ready, but that didn't make him feel secure standing out in the open like this. He could feel he was being watched as he stood there, waiting.

Not sure what to do, he started for the house. One hour had passed, but there was no sign of the caller anywhere. Experience told Stuart that the killer wouldn't show himself until the last minute and not without purpose. If Stuart kept walking, something was bound to happen.

***

Spade watched through his scope as Stuart approached the house. He waited until he was just a few feet from the front porch before reaching into his pocket and pulling out a remote detonator switch. Looking at Lance to make sure he was still watching the scene unfold, a smile played across his lips as he pressed the switch.

***

Stuart stood in front of the house, looking all around. He heard a slight hissing sound that started soft and grew in intensity. As the noise grew louder, he caught a flash of light to his left, up on the porch of the house. The flash gave way to a burning sulfur smell, and a stream of smoke blew down the planks of the rotting porch steps. Sparks began to fly, lighting the small area near the front door. Stuart could see that a box had been placed in the middle of the porch, and a folded piece of paper was taped to it.

He took one last look around before advancing on the package. Nothing else unusual had happened, but the lighting of the sparklers had not occurred randomly. The caller was close, and watching.

Removing his hands from his pockets, he placed a hand on the railing of the porch and tested the first step with his weight. Confident he wouldn't fall through; he advanced toward the box, careful to test each step before going to the next. Once on the porch, he removed the piece of paper first and tried to read it in the fading soft light of the sparklers.

Is it true that Love comes from the heart?

If so, you still hold the Love of your Wife.

Bring the bullet casing to the county bridge, or everyone dies.

You have 60 minutes. The clock is ticking.

A sick feeling welled up in his stomach as he looked down at the box. Reaching down, he picked up the box and opened it. As he did, he felt a warm sticky substance as it oozed out and covered his hands. As the last sparkler burned through its soft, cheery light, he recognized the contents. Inside the box was a human heart.

***

Kevin followed Sheriff Stone, jogging behind him out to the police cruiser. As soon as they reached the car, the sheriff turned the radio off so Kevin couldn't hear the police chatter on the designated frequency. Kevin slid in the front seat beside him and shut the door.

"We have to go back to my house."

Looking over at Kevin, he started the car and shifted into gear. He made a quick U-turn and punched the accelerator, focusing on the road ahead of him. "Why do you think that Riley made her way back to your house, Kevin?"

"My little sister was home with Mom this evening. She was there when Mom was killed. The caller said he had a package for Dad, but I don't think it was Rachelle, and I don't believe Riley thought so either. I know she overheard me on the phone. She would have gone to the house to find our sister."

Oliver Drive was eerily quiet when they made a first pass, the yellow police crime scene tape the only clue that something terrible had happened. Driving around the block and down a back alley several blocks from the house, Sheriff Jeremiah Stone found a spot to hide the police cruiser. Satisfied it wouldn't be noticed by anyone, he turned the lights off and shut the engine down before turning to Kevin.

"Where in the house do you think your sister could be hiding?"

"There is a small compartment hidden behind the paneling in the kitchen. Rachelle found it shortly after we moved in, and it became a favorite place for her to hide and play dolls. If she was afraid or heard something that frightened her, she would go down the back staircase into the kitchen and hide. I'm sure that's where she is."

"There is a good chance that the killer might return to your house, Kevin. It's not uncommon for a killer to want to go back to a crime scene and bask in what he did. There is a risk that he might be there already, so I want you to listen carefully to what I'm about to say."

Kevin's head was pounding with fear and anxiety. His mother was dead, and both of his sisters were missing. A sickness turned in his bowels as he fought down fear and forced his mind to concentrate on what needed to be done.

"I'm listening. Just tell me what to do."

"I'm going to lead the way back to your house, and we are going to enter through the back door. I know it's open because I did a walk-through when I found your mom, and the house has been taped off as a crime scene. The kitchen sits right off the back porch, right?"

"Yes. The back staircase is just to the left after you come in through the back door. There's a short hallway that leads directly into it."

"I'm going to take you to that point. You will check this compartment to see if your sister is hiding there and come directly back out to me. If she's not there, you will not go farther into the house. Do you understand?"

Kevin nodded.

"Do you understand?" Sheriff Stone demanded a verbal answer.
"Yes! I understand!" Kevin yelled back, looking angrily at him.
"Let's go then."

29

After leaving the Sheriff's office, Mark Hubbard drove over to Moses' machine shop. It was just an old renovated barn with a nice cement floor. Moses had his woodstove piping hot and Mark felt a wave of heat as he opened the side door and stepped into the shop area. It was late and typical of Moses, he was still working. Mark noticed a very nicely painted tractor loaded up on a flat bed trailer waiting to be delivered. "Hey, isn't that Siley's missing tractor?"

Moses heard Mark come in the door. It was an unexpected but very welcome visit from his best friend. "Mark! What brings your ugly butt into my fine establishment?" Moses stopped what he was working on, wiped his hands on a greasy towel and came over to visit with Mark.

"You know I didn't come to see you. I came to see that fine woman of yours, Sarah Jane. I'm here to convince her to marry me instead of your poor, sorry ass. What are you doing with Siley's tractor?"

Moses laughed at Mark's delusion. Sarah Jane was too fine of a woman to tolerate Mark's advances. Besides, all this banter was just in fun. "Charlie Joe wanted me to fix it and deliver it back to their farm before Christmas. It's ready to deliver. My cousin Brian will be here shortly to pick it up and make the delivery tonight."

The heat started getting to Mark and he unzipped his coat while he spoke. "You hear the latest news?"

"What's going on?"

"Shaun's back. He shot Neil and took Charlie Joe."

Moses' mouth dropped open. It took a moment to gather his thoughts. "You don't think he's the one who's been doin' all those killin's over in Sweetwater do ya?"

"I wouldn't put it past him, but right now he has Charlie Joe. Jeremiah thinks he's keeping her at his pappy's cabin."

"So I guess Jeremiah is on his way out there then?" Moses asked as he dropped his wrench on the bench and wiped his hands on a greasy towel.

"There's been another murder, Moses. He's over in Sweetwater helping Sheriff Langdon. He asked that you and I find CJ and make sure she's safe. Besides, Jeremiah doesn't know those woods the way you and I do."

"You got your gun?"

"It's in the truck. I'll wait for you to get yours. Engine's running."

30

Sweetwater, Missouri

Stuart Riedel and Sheriff Langdon met back at the car at the end of the driveway. Handing the piece of paper to the sheriff, Stuart carefully laid the box on the floor in the backseat of the car. Clear resolve overtook any other emotion, and he now knew he would have the chance to face the person who murdered his wife. Taking the gun from the front seat and securing it back into the holster at his side, he closed the door and waited.

FBI Agent Engel approached the car from the road, having been stationed in the dense timber on the north side of the abandoned house. Sheriff Langdon passed the message to Engel and turned to Stuart.

"Do you have the bullet casing that he wants, Stuart?"

"It's back at the office in the evidence box."

Sheriff Langdon radioed out to his men, ordering two to search the area for any evidence they might find that the caller had been at the scene. The fireworks display had been triggered, meaning he was somewhere nearby, or at least had been. One officer was given a key to the sheriff's office, with instructions on where to find the bullet casing. Ten men stood available, ready to secure the next rendezvous point.

Pulling the map out again, Sheriff Langdon began instructing his men on the geographical challenges of the next assignment.

"The Missouri River runs wide and deep at the point that it flows under the county bridge. The drop from the top of the bridge to the water below is approximately eighty feet. It's possible that the caller may use the water as a means of escape. The greater probability is the access to I-70 straight south. I want a roadblock set up on both sides of the bridge, with a man watching the water."

FBI Agent Engel placed a call asking for backup in Platte County at the access point to the interstate highway. They didn't know exactly what they were looking for at this point, but any vehicles with out-of-county tags should be stopped. The man they were looking for was known as Spade and should be considered armed and dangerous. He could have one, perhaps two hostages, one being a small child.

Stuart watched and listened as these two men gave their orders, executing a plan that he wasn't sure he wanted to survive. He wasn't afraid of his own death, but he was worried about the safety of his family. Shirley was gone, but he still had three kids to care for. He couldn't just give up. He had to hang on for them. He had to. All his life he'd been a cop, and he always knew that his family was safe and secure at home while he struggled against the evils of this world to make it a safer place, a better place. Now evil had come to rest upon his family, and it took every fiber of courage to step forward. Standing against the storm that raged and battered against the walls of his faith, he bound up his soul with the words of the twenty-third psalm and with renewed confidence he turned to these soldiers before him.

"Let's rock and roll. We have an appointment to keep."

***

Sheriff Jeremiah Stone entered the back door first, gun drawn. The house was dark and appeared to be undisturbed from when the police had vacated it just an hour earlier. Moving along the wall, he checked the staircase first before moving toward the kitchen. The house was quiet. Kevin was close behind him. Ensuring the kitchen was clear, Sheriff Stone relaxed and turned to Kevin, watching him as he felt along the paneling near the floor.

When Kevin pressed against the wall, a door clicked and hinged quietly open, revealing a small, dark compartment. Kevin knelt down and placed his elbows on the floor as he looked in at Rachelle, softly calling her name. She had fallen asleep on her side, a decorative box he'd never seen before and her favorite doll clutched to her chest.

Hearing Kevin's voice, she opened her eyes, and seeing him, she scrambled out of her hiding place. Tightfisting her box and doll, she tumbled into his arms. Great sobs of relief choked her as she clung to his neck.

Stroking her back, Kevin picked her up and started toward the back door. "You're OK now, Rachelle. I have you. You're safe," he whispered into her ear.

Sheriff Jeremiah Stone struggled to control his own emotions as he listened to Kevin quietly calming Rachelle. Composing himself, he guided the two back down the alley and into the police cruiser. Kevin hugged her to his chest, mindful of her head as he lowered himself into the front seat. Sheriff Stone walked back to the trunk to retrieve a blanket for them. The shock of what Rachelle had gone through was sure to cause her temperature to drop. Keeping her warm until he was able to get her to the hospital was important at this point. He wanted to make sure that she wasn't hurt and that she was kept safe until this ordeal was over.

Sliding in behind the wheel, he turned the car back toward the closest hospital in Kansas City. The police radio was still off, and Sheriff Stone had no idea what awaited them at the bridge they had to cross to reach the hospital.

***

The white Hummer had been parked on a side road and the night equipment unloaded. Lance watched as Spade worked quietly and methodically. The rifle, night goggles, and other small bundles of equipment were packed and quickly shouldered.

Satisfied that everything necessary had been stowed for easy retrieval, Spade opened the back door of the Hummer and moved the tarp that covered Riley's body. Pulling her out by her feet, he dropped her unceremoniously to the ground. Spade grabbed her by her arms and dragged her forward so that she leaned up against the back tire. He checked her pulse and made sure she was still breathing before opening a small leather case and preparing a vial for injection.

"What are you doing?"

Looking up at Lance, Spade smiled and stabbed the long needle into her thigh through her jeans, injecting the full syringe into her muscle. "We don't want the princess to wake up and cause us trouble now, do we?" He gently laughed. "It might spoil our fun!"

Standing up and shifting the weight of his pack, he reached back down and lifted Riley onto his shoulder like a rag doll. Without looking back to see if Lance followed, he strode across the rocky pasture toward the highway.

Lance watched him walking off into the night. He had thought that Spade would kill Riley's dad back at the abandoned house, but the man was beyond insane. He seemed to enjoy the thrill of being chased, and the rules of the game changed at whim as the night unfolded. He was unpredictable and totally dangerous. Lance could run now. Spade was too focused and enjoyed this game too much to take much heed of him running, but then there was Riley. He couldn't leave her. It was his fault that she was mixed up in this. Her only crime was believing in him. He couldn't do that to her. *I can't just leave her*, he thought as he picked up the canvas pack and followed them.

31

Sweetwater, Missouri

Traffic on County Road 1012 was normally light this time of night. Sheriff Langdon had set up patrol blocks a quarter mile north and south of the bridge to ensure no traffic was allowed through. Stuart parked his police car on the north end of the bridge, leaving his lights on to illuminate the long corridor before him. Standing there in the moonlight, he could hear the rushing water below. He had always hated this bridge. It was narrow and long, and the drop to the water below was tremendous.

The bullet casing the caller had asked for was in Stuart's pocket. He carried the crossbow this time. A quiver of metal arrows hung over his shoulder and one was loaded into the crossbow ready to fire. Looking at his watch, he saw his team had a full ten minutes to finish getting into place and preparing before the deadline. His adrenaline was rushing. As he allowed his police training to kick in, his mind began to tick through possible scenarios and how to handle them. Having a plan and knowing how to react calmed his nerves and changed his focus. He knew that FBI Agent Engel and Sheriff Langdon were somewhere to his left and right, hidden in the rocky crags of the surrounding terrain. This part of Missouri had a lot of ravines and thick timber that abruptly ended at open fields. It was perfect cover for wildlife, creating a challenging hunting environment for those who enjoyed the sport. As far as police work went, it provided too much opportunity for a killer to maneuver. Stuart tried not to focus on this small point. Instead he focused on the road ahead.

***

Sheriff Jeremiah Stone reached the blockade at the north end of the bridge just as the police were exiting their vehicles to stop traffic from flowing through. A little red Mazda Miata idled in front of him as an officer asked for identification, then instructed the driver to turn around and leave the area. Pulling forward to the side of the road, he shut the police cruiser off and went to see what was going on.

Kevin remained in the car, still focusing on Rachelle. She hadn't said anything to him, and her eyes were a bit glazed over. She still held tight to her doll, and a small decorative box that she had with her when he found her. Her hand rested on his chest, her fingers outlining the square object in his coat pocket. He had forgotten he still had Riley's phone. Shifting her weight, she sat up a little bit, and then leaned back against him. He held her gently, rubbing her back, trying to get her to relax again. His own mind played back over the evening. He regretted hitting Mr. Nelson for trying to stop him from leaving. Riley still was missing. *Riley.*

Kevin sat up straighter as his mind began playing back over that moment. He had given her his phone to keep. If she still had it on her, they could locate her with the GPS system. All they had to do was call the carrier, and they could pinpoint her location to within a few feet. Excitement grew as he opened the door and sat Rachelle down in the seat, covering her with the blanket.

"I'll be right back, Rachelle. You stay here, OK?" he said before closing the door.

Sheriff Jeremiah Stone heard the car door open and turned to see Kevin getting out. Sure that Kevin was up to something, he wanted to nip it in the bud quickly before the teenager got out of control. The last thing he wanted to do tonight was to handcuff the kid, but if it came to that, he would do it to keep him safe.

"Kevin, get back in the car now!" he ordered.

Kevin ignored him, and as he came forward, he reached into his coat pocket. Alarmed, the other officers reached for their guns as Sheriff Stone advanced on him. Everyone's nerves were a bit raw, and they were ready to react.

Pulling out his phone, he handed it to Sheriff Stone. "She may still have the phone on her. I gave it to her back at the Nelsons' house." Seeing that Sheriff Stone didn't understand, he started over. "My sister, Riley. She's still missing. The last time I saw her, I gave her my phone to keep. It has a GPS system on it. If you call the carrier, you might be able to locate her position."

***

Spade stopped the vehicle a quarter of a mile south of bridge on County Road 1012 leaving Lance in the middle of the road with an unconscious Riley. His canvas pack had been taken from him, and he had been instructed to carry her to the middle of the road. An earpiece and microphone were attached to him so Spade could hear the exchange: Riley for the bullet casing. A cable had been secured to the side of the bridge, and once the exchange had taken place, Lance was to attach the harness that he wore to the cable, lowering himself to the water below. He would run out of cable twenty feet above the water, dropping into the river and letting the current carry him forward to the raft. If all went well, Spade would pick him up in the raft and motor him to a point downriver, where they would commandeer a vehicle.

The problem was that Lance had never learned to swim. There was no way he was going over the bridge and into the water. He had no idea how far below the Missouri River was, but just the sound of the water rushing by caused him to sweat. Knowing that Spade could hear every word, and that he now hid in the shadows with a high-power rifle, Lance took a deep breath and reached down to pick up Riley.

Her small, limp frame was heavy in his arms—dead weight that was difficult to manage in the long walk to the middle of the bridge. He could see the headlights of the car at the other end. The shifting shadows in the light cast the image of a tall man walking toward him. With the weight of Riley growing heavier in his arms, Lance thought back to all the things he had done wrong in his life, and how he could have done things differently. His mom worked a lot, and his own dad was in prison, but that didn't mean he had to make the choices he had made. He didn't have to run drugs to Wichita. It certainly didn't profit him, and in the end, all it came to was death. It seemed to surround him, and he knew as he walked toward Stuart, that he had little chance of coming out of this alive. He had one chance to make a difference here. Once chance to make what he'd done right again. He only hoped that Riley could one day forgive him for what he'd done to her family. She had been a light in his life, a hope he didn't even know he needed until he met her.

Reaching the middle of the bridge, he stopped and gently laid Riley down on the centerline. Looking up into the sky, Lance could see the Big Dipper boldly glowing above him. The water rushing below drowned out the rest of the night noises. Taking a deep breath, he looked up and faced her dad. He stood only a few feet away.

"She's been drugged, Mr. Riedel. She's OK. He didn't hurt her."

Stuart was a little shocked to see Riley in the road instead of Rachelle. He hadn't known Riley was missing, and now he worried that Rachelle was dead too. Calming himself, he forced his mind back to the task before him, noticing the sadness in the boy's eyes for the first time. He was just a kid, caught up in a dangerous game. He wondered if he really ever understood the ramifications of his decisions. Most kids didn't until it was too late. How could they, when there wasn't anyone around to guide them, to help them when they needed it? Stuart was no stranger to the side of life that Lance had lived. He'd seen it over and over in his career, and when he could, he tried to make a difference.

A phone rang, startling Lance. He looked up at Stuart to see what he should do. Stuart nodded to him as if to indicate he should answer it.

Without knowing what else to do, he reached into Riley's coat pocket and answered the phone.

"Hello?"

The soft, hollow sound of a bullet impacting flesh echoed around Stuart. He didn't know where it came from as his eyes quickly scanned everything around him. A small line of blood cascaded from the boy's shoulder; blood created an ever-growing circle onto his jacket as he stood there holding the phone. He looked up at Stuart for just a moment before his knees buckled, and he dropped forward onto the pavement, partially covering Riley. Lunging forward to cover them, Stuart raised his crossbow and searched the darkness for clues.

His eyes scanned the area, but he couldn't see anyone or anything beyond the cement railing of the bridge. His eyes fell back to the boy. Lance was still alive. For the first time, Stuart saw the microphone and earpiece the boy had been wearing. Reaching over his body, he took the earpiece off of Lance and put the earpiece in his own ear and then pinned the microphone to his shirt.

"Just you and me, Spade. Be a man and come out in the open to play with someone your own size," he taunted, crossbow drawn and ready to kill.

***

Kevin watched as Sheriff Stone made radio contact with Sheriff Langdon. The call had been authorized, and they now knew that Riley was on the bridge with his dad. Shots had been fired, and all but one officer had scattered to support and back up Detective Stuart on the bridge. The darkness greatly impeded their ability to provide defense and long-range protection. Kevin didn't like the idea of his dad out on that bridge alone with Riley. At the very least, he could sneak out and bring Riley back in to safety, leaving his dad free to focus on the killer.

"Hold on, Kevin. Get back in the car and stay there." Sheriff Jeremiah Stone had been watching Kevin closely.

"I have to help if I can. You can't stop me."

Sheriff Stone walked over to Kevin and grabbed him by the wrist. He twisted his arm behind Kevin's back and strong-armed him towards the patrol car without saying a word. Once at the car, Sheriff Stone handcuffed him to the passenger door. Without looking back, Sheriff Stone strode over to Detective Stuart's car and spoke with one of the officers. Kevin watched as Sheriff Stone donned a pair of night vision goggles. He carried a high-power rifle with him as he strode over to the edge of the bridge and began climbing the railing upwards.

Holy shit. He's climbing the bridge for a vantage point on the killer, Kevin thought. *If he falls, he's dead.*

***

Spade crouched within the underbrush off the western side of the river. He had a clear shot of Detective Riedel, but he loved hearing the angry challenge as it came over the headphones. *Ingenious of him to take the bug off the kid and use it to taunt him,* Spade thought. Detective Riedel was proving to be a worthy foe. It had been a long time since he'd had this much fun on a kill, and he wanted to prolong it as much as possible.

Placing the rifle on the ground next to him, he pulled on the night-vision goggles to count the officers stationed in the underbrush around him. Three were clearly visible within one hundred yards of him. Moving slowly and quietly, he began his descent toward the undercarriage of the bridge. New players to the game would require changes in his plans in order to keep things spicy and interesting. Retrieving the bullet casing was no longer the only goal for Spade. *The thrill of this hunt is intoxicating!*

***

Climbing the bridge trestles allowed Sheriff Stone a distinct advantage on Shaun, aka Spade. Sheriff Stone told Detective Riedel who he thought the killer was, but he still didn't know why he was targeting the detective, or why Charlie Joe was taken hostage. He had been remiss in not telling Sheriff Langdon what he knew, but there had never been a good time for that to happen. At this point in the game, though, it didn't matter. He knew Shaun. He knew how he hunted. Patience was the key to winning this game.

Shaun had not been present on the bridge as anticipated. Based on the shot that injured Lance, he was south and west of the bridge. It had been more than ten minutes since that shot had been fired, and Sheriff Stone was trying to calculate Shaun's next movement. Detective Riedel had taken the microphone off of Lance and could be heard communicating with Shaun. It was funny how sound carried over water. It's echo made it difficult to locate the origin of the sound, so it was important to focus on light, movement and shadow. Shaun found a comfortable position and nestled against the cold steel of the bridge trellis. Once that was done, his hands were free to scour the timberline with his high-grade night vision goggles.

***

Stuart Riedel had to be careful. The microphone he had taken off of Lance was picking everything he said or was said around him. That meant that Spade could hear what was going on. He looked Lance in the eyes and mouthed "Are you okay?"

Lance nodded indicating that yes, he was okay. Stuart knew it was a lie, but the fact that Lance was able to respond was encouraging.

A police car inched along the bridge from the north towards them to help provide cover so that Lance and Riley could be removed from the line of fire. Once the car was fifty feet from them, bullets began coming at them. All three stayed as flat to the surface of the road as they could, waiting for the bullet spray to stop. The car reached them a few seconds later, creating enough cover for Stuart to load Lance and Riley into the car. Bullets continued to spray from the south-west side of the bridge.

Dear God, please help us get out of this alive, Stuart prayed.

32

The bullet spray was a gift Sheriff Jeremiah Stone had not expected from Shaun. *Impatient tonight, ol' buddy?* he thought. *Or is the thrill of this hunt a bit much for you?*

He zeroed in on Shaun's location and was about to take a shot when Shaun effectively ducked back into the timberline. Jeremiah would have to act more quickly if he expected to get a hit. He really only had one chance to do this and do it right. Once he made his shot, his cover would be blown and Shaun would be able to retaliate with a kill shot. It was a risk but one he was willing to take.

***

"Call an ambulance. Lance is injured and Riley is unconscious," Detective Stuart Riedel ordered as he passed the officer on the north end of the bridge and headed toward his car. Stuart opened his car door and shut off the headlights, allowing the darkness to consume the bridge once more.

Sheriff Langdon came up out of the underbrush to the east of the road with a high-power rifle in his hands.

"I caught a glimpse of him on the south-west side when he fired those shots, Stuart, and radioed his position to the men there. I haven't received any call back, though, so we don't know his current position. It's pretty safe to assume he can't cross that water without being seen by my men on the shore, and he won't be crossing the bridge on foot. Let's take a breath here and consider our options."

Stuart leaned against the squad car, looking back he saw Kevin handcuffed to the police car. Riley had been drugged, and Lance was injured but still alive. That was a measure of relief, but the night wasn't over yet.

"I want an officer to get Kevin and Riley as far away from here as possible. My youngest daughter is still missing, Sheriff."

"We found her in the cupboard at home, dad," Kevin assured him. "Sheriff Stone was en route to take us to the hospital when we came upon the barricade here. She's in the car."

Relief and fear washed over Stuart at the same moment. All three of his kids were safe, but they all three were in the middle of a manhunt. The sooner they were out of here, the safer they would be. Knowing that the ambulance would take a good twenty minutes to reach them, he looked around at the police standing here with him. He only knew Sheriff Langdon. Sheriff Stone seemed to be a good man but was nowhere to be seen at the moment. Deputy Sheriff Jordan Morey worked over in Blackhorse with Sheriff Jeremiah Stone. Sheriff Langdon knew him well, but the other officer was unfamiliar to him. Stuart knew that eight others, including Special Agents Engel and Dime, were working reconnaissance in the timber on each side of the bridge.

The question now was what would the killer do next. What was his next move going to be?

"We are dealing with a serial killer here. Sheriff Stone has a theory that the killer is someone from his county. A man named Shaun Lemoine," Stuart offered. "Profiles on these types of men generally identify a white male under the age of thirty-five. They are calculated and enjoy the thrill of the kill, often wanting to see the victim and watch them die firsthand. This description fits the man Sheriff Stone identified. Most likely, because he shot Lance on the bridge, he has sophisticated equipment that allows him to watch from afar. He had this whole takedown planned down to the escape route, but because we are no longer on the bridge, he has to reformulate his next move. The imbalance of the operation is going to cause him to become more reckless and thus more dangerous. The one advantage he has right now is that he grew up in this area and knows these woods very well. He apparently hunted them with his father."

"I know Shaun Lemoine. He was dangerous as a kid. If he's the one doing the killings here, he is extremely dangerous. Smart. Creative. Don't underestimate him," Sheriff Langdon said. "We found a raft tied to the pillar of the bridge in the middle of the river. It's been removed, but we can't discount that he may take to the water and try to escape tonight without further engagement."

"No, we can't afford to eliminate any options right now. Let's consider other possibilities. Either of you two officers have an opinion?"

Looking back at Stuart, Deputy Sheriff Jordan Morey thought a moment before offering his opinion. "I don't believe he'll just escape, to be honest. He has a taste for killing, and from what I've read about serial killers, they tend to lose their ability to control as their desire increases. He'll take more risks tonight. It's no longer about getting the evidence. I think he saw another man on the bridge and allowed Stuart to leave with Riley to increase the stakes. It's the thrill of the hunt he wants. The man is intelligent, and we need to prepare for the unexpected."

"Sheriff, why don't you radio each of your men," Stuart said. "Let's get confirmation on everyone's position before we plan our next move."

An officer came out of the timber abruptly to the right of Stuart. He was a large man and clearly had struggled through the underbrush, tearing his uniform in several places and causing an unusual amount of blood to stain the front of his shirt and pants. Stuart watched him limp towards the bridge. Stuart turned his attention back to Deputy Sheriff Jordan Morey as Sheriff Langdon began radioing each officer's position on the designated frequency.

"I have some coffee back in my car, Detective, if you care for something to drink," Deputy Sheriff Jordan Morey offered. "Rachelle is there. She might feel better if she could see you for a moment. We are still waiting for the ambulance to come for Riley and Lance. They are still in the lead car up ahead. I just checked on them. Riley is awake now and seems to be okay. I have a pressure dressing on Lance's wound. The bleeding has slowed down. He's still awake and talking to Riley."

Knowing that he had a few minutes and that Rachelle would give him as much comfort as he would give her, he accepted the deputy's hospitality and followed him back to the police car.

Rachelle lay in the backseat, covered with a navy-blue, wool, police-issue blanket. He appreciated the fact that the officer had taken the time to give her some comfort in this horrific ordeal. He opened the door to the backseat and gently lifted Rachelle onto his lap, holding her close to himself and smelling the sweetness of her hair. She stirred only to find a warm and more comfortable position, never fully opening her eyes. It was not uncommon for small children to sleep during periods of high stress. Their little brains could not fully process the horrors they were sometimes exposed to and as a measure of survival, they just shut down and slept.

Stuart had held her but a few moments when Sheriff Langdon approached. Laying her gently back on to the backseat of the car, he locked the door and softly closed it before acknowledging the sheriff.

"Agent Dime and one other officer haven't responded to my radio call, Stuart," he said. It was clear that Sheriff Langdon, although he had been an officer his entire life, was relying heavily on Stuart for guidance in this ordeal.

"You have five men, four whose positions in the field are known?"

"Correct," Sheriff Langdon answered.

"Who's the officer over there by Deputy Sheriff Jordan Morey? He should be your fifth man that you are missing. I watched him walk out of the timber and up onto the bridge a little while ago."

Sheriff Langdon took a long look at the very tall man standing by the deputy sheriff. Something was off about him. He didn't know why, but his instincts were telling him something was wrong.

Baffled and slightly intimidated by the events of the evening, Sheriff Langdon questioned himself. "It's been a long night. I'll call the officer over and talk to him," he admitted. Directing his attention to one of the officers near the blockade, he instructed him to make another call out to confirm positions and then called the unknown officer over to their position by the car.

33

The glass edge of the broken peach jar cut through the ropes that bound Charlie Joe. She was able to get herself free but her hands remained numb and her eye remained swollen shut. Her head was pounding and she was freezing cold. Her limbs were stiff, and moving was difficult. It didn't help that she was fighting the urge to sleep. All she really wanted to do was lay down and close her eyes, but fear drove her. She knew Shaun would come back for her, and that was certain death.

She wiped the blood from her foot off of her skin with her sock before putting it back on. The wound was deeper than she thought, but it didn't appear that there was any glass in it. She winced with pain as she pulled her boot back on and stood up in the low cellar. Looking around, she could see the stairwell in the shadows. Her only two options of escape were the small window or the cellar door. *Knowing Shaun, the door would be chained from the outside. He was a man of details. He always paid attention to details. I seriously doubt that has changed over the years.*

Without trying the cellar door, Charlie Joe walked stooped over towards the window. It was small, but she thought she would be able to squeeze through easy enough. She found a brick on the floor next to the wall. A burlap sack hung on a nail next to the peaches. She wrapped the burlap sack around her hand and forearm, picked the brick up and smashed out the windowpane. Cold air rushed in as the glass shattered. Moon shadows danced across the timbered floor. Looking up into the night sky, Charlie Joe could see clouds blowing in. The wind was picking up, too.

She placed the burlap sack over the broken glass and pulled herself up into the window frame. It was tight and her shirt caught on a glass shard, ripping the fabric. She crawled out onto the frozen ground. Leaves blew past her as she rolled over onto her back.

She lay there, listening for a minute, trying to decide which direction she should go. The only sounds she heard were the hooting of an owl and wind through the trees. *No cars. There has to be a road around here somewhere, but taking it is risky. Old Man Lemoine was crazy. He was suspicious of everyone and if the stories are true, there are traps all around this cabin.* The coldness from the frozen earth began seeping into her skin. Charlie Joe sat up and looked around her. All she had on was a thin jacket. She had to move to stay warm, and putting distance between her and this cabin was a priority. Not knowing which direction she was headed, she took to the tree line and prayed. *Lord, I need you to guide my footsteps. Please send an angel to help me.*

As she stepped into the timberline, she heard a snap and instantly her head felt like it was going to explode. Everything went black again.

34

Sweetwater, Missouri

Sheriff Jeremiah Stone, from his position on the bridge trestle, watched as an officer emerged from the timberline and advanced towards the road north of the bridge. Sheriff Langdon and FBI Agent Dixon, the agent in charge, had not placed an officer in that area. Refocusing his night vision goggles, he zoned in on the officer's face and immediate recognition hit him. Shaun was wearing a police uniform. Pulling his rifle up to take aim, he watched as Shaun began jogging in a zig-zag, then slowed as he advanced on a small group of officers that were standing on the bridge. *Detective Stuart Riedel is behind Shaun now. He knows his position. He's going to kill Stuart on the bridge,* Sheriff Stone thought as realized he would never have a clear shot now. He began to rapidly climb to the bridge floor as fast as he could. *I've only got seconds. This is going down now.*

***

Riley opened her eyes to see Lance propped up against the inside of the car door. A towel was taped to his chest and she could see blood all over his shirt. He was breathing hard, and not moving but his eyes were open and staring out the window. Realization hit her as she began to remember what had happened.

"Lance! Are you okay?"

"I've been shot, Riley," he panted. *The bullet must have grazed my lung,* he thought. He closed his eyes as he caught his breath before he tried to continue. "Spade is outside on the bridge, Riley. I can hear him."

Riley scooted across the back seat of the police cruiser and looked directly at him. Lance turned to face her. "Riley, seriously. This man is going to kill us."

Riley followed his gaze out the window. She could hear her dad and Sheriff Langdon talking but couldn't understand what they were saying.

"See your dad, Riley? Look at the officer just beyond him. He just joined the group. It's Spade. He's hunting your dad. When he's done killing him, he'll come for us."

Looking out the window, Riley saw what Lance was talking about. Spade was a very tall man: taller than anyone else on the bridge. "Dad doesn't know what's going on, Lance. I have to help him." Riley touched the gun in the pocket of her coat that she had taken from Janet's house. It was still there. Anger, fear and courage melted together as she quietly opened the car door and slipped out on to pavement.

Kevin was a few feet away from her, to her right. He looked up at her just as she was crouching next to the door and gently closing it. Seeing him, Riley touched her lips with her index finger and shook her head 'no.' *Kevin, you have to keep quiet for this to work*, she thought.

Creeping along the side of the car, Riley pulled the gun out, flipped the safety to the off position just as Janet had shown her, stood and took aim at the officer just beyond where her dad was standing.

35

Blackhorse, Missouri

Mark Hubbard drove the truck down the low-maintenance road. Moses rode shotgun giving Mark directions to the Lemoine hunting cabin. To some folks, this dirt track wouldn't be considered passable, let alone a road, but in a four-wheel drive pick up truck, it was manageable though bumpy and slow going. A car would have trouble on a road like this.

"You sure we're headed in the right direction, Moses? I thought the cabin was close to the lake," Mark asked.

"Most people assume that, and that's what Ol' Man Lemoine wanted people to think. He liked his privacy and less people knew about him the better. His boys take after him in that regard."

Just then, Mark slammed on the breaks. A huge tree loomed in the middle of the road, effectively ending it. "What the hell?" Mark yelled.

"This is the end of the line, my friend. The cabin is a two mile walk from here." Moses reached behind the seat and grabbed a flashlight before opening his door. The wind began to howl, and clouds were blowing in. "I can smell snow in the air. We best get moving. No tellin' how we are going to find Charlie Joe."

Mark grabbed a flashlight from under his seat along with his Smith & Wessen handgun. He wasn't going into these woods without a gun knowing that Shaun could be in the area. He closed the truck door and followed Moses through the dense underbrush. "No trails?"

"Nope. No trails. Just follow me and watch your step."

After an hour of walking, they came upon a small clearing and Mark could see an outline of a rough cabin in the fading moonlight. The night was getting colder. Moses didn't seem to mind the cold as he advanced on the cabin and gained the front porch steps.

"Charlie Joe?" Moses softly called as he opened the cabin door and stepped inside.

Mark stayed in the yard, watching the timberline for intruders. The wind was moving the trees quite a bit. *No one's going to live out here for very long in this cold.*

Moses stepped back out onto the porch. "No one's inside. I'll go around and check the cellar. He may have tied her up down there."

Mark didn't respond other than to walk around to the other side of the cabin. He noticed a broken window and a torn piece of fabric swaying on the edge of the broken glass. "Moses!" he yelled.

Moses came around to the side of the house near Mark and immediately saw the broken glass in the beam of Mark's flashlight. "She was here. Looks like she was able to get out, but where would she have gone?"

Moses turned his attention to the timberline. "Ol' Man Lemoine was crazy. He hated people. If stories are true, he set traps all around this area to keep intruders out."

Mark stood there, listening. "Ol' Man Lemoine has been dead for years. You think those traps are still set?"

"Shaun is just like his pappy. The inside of that cabin was well stocked and clean as a pin. My guess is that he took to these woods and reset all of the traps his pappy had just to make sure that no one would intrude without his knowing. That would be a best case scenario."

"I'm not sure what you mean, Moses."

"Remember back in the summer of 1994?"

"Charlie Joe and Jeremiah got caught stealing watermelons that summer."

"That wasn't the only thing that happened that summer, Mark. Ol' Man Lemoine was angry at Shaun for not torturing a fox after shooting it. I remember this distinctly because I was home the night this happened. It was the only time I ever saw their momma alive."

"What happened, Moses?"

"Ol' Man Lemoine decided he had had enough of Shaun's insolence so he beat Neil to unconsciousness and tied him to the railroad tracks to teach Shaun a lesson." The memory brought tears to the brim of Moses' eyes, but he held them back. He took a deep breath, but his voice caught as he continued. "He made Shaun watch the whole thing. As the train was coming down the tracks, Shaun broke free of his pappy and cut the bailing twine that held his brother down. As he rolled Neil away from the rail, a metal pin on the front of the train caught Shaun's shirt and tore his chest open before flipping him off to the side. He was still conscious when his pappy grabbed him and beat him for saving Neil. Their Momma brought the boys to our house that night. She didn't have money to take them to a doctor."

"Jesus, Moses."

"Jesus was there that night, Mark. No doubt about it. It was an act of God that either one of them lived."

A strange shape caught Moses' eye as he spoke. He started walking towards it, careful to watch where he stepped. "Is that what I think it is?" he asked.

Mark followed his flashlight beam with his eyes. "Looks like a broken branch hanging from a tree to me."

Moses walked closer and began to make out a body swinging from a tree. A noose had wrapped around her ankle and in the narrow beam of his flashlight, Moses could see that Charlie Joe was swinging upside down ten feet off of the ground. He couldn't tell if she was dead or alive. Her face was swollen and purple. She wasn't moving. "Get your knife, Mark! Hurry!"

36

"Yes sir," the unknown officer said, following the sheriff back toward Stuart. The officer had effectively placed himself between Stuart and the twins. Rachelle was still in the car, sleeping. Stuart's back was to his children as he watched the officer walk towards him. This was the same officer whose uniform was torn and blood stained. Stuart's instincts were screaming that something was wrong.

"What is he doing?" Stuart wondered aloud as he watched him move closer.

The officer stopped suddenly just a few feet from Stuart, and turned his back to him as if to pull a pad of paper from his back pocket and radio out to confirm positions. Stuart relaxed slightly as he kept a close eye on this officer. Something just wasn't right. He should move away from people to hear more effectively.

"Stuart, did you hear me?" Sheriff Langdon asked again.

"What?"

"Agent Engel just radioed in that another group of agents are on their way here for backup. The ambulance should be here in another five minutes."

Looking back at Sheriff Langdon, Stuart caught Jeremiah's movements out of the corner of his eye. *Why is Jeremiah climbing down the bridge trellis?* Stuart thought. Then he realized the killer had infiltrated their group and was preparing to attack.

Moving as if in slow motion, Shaun, *aka Spade in uniform* pulled his gun from the holster, turned and aimed his gun point-blank at Stuart's chest. A shot rang out and reflexively Stuart jumped backwards onto the hood of the police car. Another shot sounded as Stuart watched Spade fall on to the pavement just a few feet in front of him.

Jeremiah was on the scene instantly, rifle ready and pointed directly at Shaun's head.

"Stuart, are you okay?" Jeremiah asked. "Were you hit? Where did the shots come from?"

Stuart bent down and turned Spade's body over. Two shots to the heart. Direct hit. He wasn't dead yet, but he was bleeding out fast. Without answering Jeremiah, Stuart turned and looked behind him. Riley stood there, shaking. Holding a gun. Eyes wide open. Jaw dropped. He walked over to her and without saying a word, he took the gun from her hands and wrapped her in a bear hug. Holding her tight. She began to sob.

"He was going to kill you, dad."

"It's okay, Riley. Everything's going to be okay."

37

County Hospital, Missouri

County Hospital started out as a small fifty-bed healthcare facility. As the surrounding populations grew, additions to the hospital were built to accommodate the growing need. The bright red Emergency sign on the entrance was part of the new edition and could be seen from the highway. Several ambulances lined up along the entrance and teams of healthcare workers swarmed the area, each focusing on the patients as they were unloaded. Sheriff Jeremiah Stone could make out Lance, the young man who had been shot in the lung and Detective Riedel's oldest boy, Kevin and his twin sister Riley. Several police officers from Blackhorse were milling around, creating a perimeter to keep the newscast at bay. Channel 2 News and Channel 8 News were competing for the breaking story. Sheriff Stone drove around to the side entrance of the emergency room to park and slipped in without being noticed.

Sheriff Jeremiah Stone knew Charlie Joe had arrived at the hospital already, but he didn't know where she was. Mark Hubbard had called him enroute to the hospital. Jeremiah was still on the bridge watching paramedics pronounce Shaun dead and placing him in a body bag when he received Mark's call.

"She's alive, Jeremiah, but we can't wake her up. She's been beat pretty badly. Moses carried her out of the woods to the truck and we are taking her to the hospital now."

Sheriff Stone had left the bridge immediately after receiving the call. Now, standing in the emergency room, he wasn't sure how to find her. A short thin woman with black hair in scrubs stood at the nurse's station, taking rapidly on the phone. As Sheriff Stone approached her, he could hear her conversation.

"Concussion. No intracranial hemorrhaging per CT. Fractured mandible. Compound fracture of the femur and four broken ribs.

We've typed and cross-matched for a blood transfusion and are prepping her for surgery now. Anesthesia was in house and has already seen her. The OR team has been called in for you." The woman paused while she listened, noticing Sheriff Stone standing close to her. She turned her back to him before she continued. "The boy is seventeen years old. He has a fractured clavicle and collapsed lung and is headed in for surgery now with Dr. Voslam. I'll tell them you are on your way." Hanging up the phone, the dark haired woman turned to Sheriff Stone, annoyed. "We are busy. What do you need?"

"I'm looking for a young woman who came in by private vehicle. Her name is Charlie Joe Bingham."

"Are you relation?"

"I'm all the relation she has," Jeremiah responded.

"My name is Dr. Hamid. Miss Bingham is headed to surgery. She's in Bay 4 if you want to sit with her for a few minutes. She is beaten up pretty badly and is in and out of consciousness, but she will be able to hear your voice." She picked up another chart and began working her way towards Bay 2 in the emergency room without waiting for Sheriff Stone to respond.

Jeremiah watched her for a moment before he turned and saw the bay numbers on the wall. Bay 4's glass door was partially open but the curtain was pulled. He strode to the curtain and pulled it back to see two nurses working on Charlie Joe. Her face was unrecognizable, her breathing raspy and uneven. He could see that she was struggling to stay alive. Emotions overtook him and tears spilled over uncontrollably. He stood next to the gurney she laid upon and took her hand. He stroked her fingers as he watched her face.

"We've given her Demerol to help control the pain. She's pretty out of it, but she can still hear you," the nurse offered.

"Hey, CJ. I'm here. I'm not leaving. I'm here," he whispered.

CJ squeezed his hand as he stroked her fingers. Tears blinded him as he began to silently pray. *Holy Father, please hear me now. C.J is the*

*one person on this earth that I can't live without. I love her with all my
heart. You've protected her and kept her in the palm of your hand this day.
Please be with her now as well. Be with the surgeon who will work on her
broken body. Heal her, Lord. Bring her back to me. In Christ's name I
pray and entrust her to you.*

***

The curtain at the foot of the gurney moved and a short, thin man
wearing high tops entered the room. Dr. David Sousa had just finished
playing a pick up basketball game with his two boys at the local gym
when he was paged about the shootings on the bridge. A second page
about a young woman found hanging upside down in a tree had come
just seconds after the first. Dr. Voslam was a young surgeon, but
extremely talented. He was able to get to the hospital first, and took
a young man named Lance Meton into operating room number three.
Given the scope of Miss Bingham's injuries, Dr. Sousa had been chosen
to begin working on her. Dr. Voslam would join him after finishing
with his own patient.

"My name is Dr. Sousa. I'm taking Miss Bingham to surgery in a
few minutes." He offered his hand to Jeremiah as he spoke.

Jeremiah shook his hand, but his emotions were running too high
to say anything. Tears clung to his eyelashes.

Dr. Sousa turned his focus onto Charlie Joe. "Good evening, Ms.
Bingham. It appears you've had a bad day," he offered. Humor in the
face of tragedy helped alleviate some of the trauma, if only for a
moment.

Charlie Joe didn't respond to Dr. Sousa as he took a penlight out
and checked her pupils. He listened to her heart, lungs and abdomen
with his Littman stethoscope before turning back to Jeremiah. "Are you
her husband?"

"No. I'm the closest relation she has at this moment," Jeremiah said.

"She's in pretty bad shape. I'm taking her to surgery now. It likely will be a long surgery given the scope of her injuries. She has a concussion and her jaw is broken. She also has four broken ribs rubbing against her lung tissue causing problems with her breathing. We have to correct that before her lungs are punctured and collapse. Her femur is broken as well. The nurses will get your contact information so that I can call you and give you a status update if you want to go home and rest for awhile," Dr. Sousa offered. The Sheriff looked haggard and about to collapse himself.

"I'm not leaving, doctor. I'll be right here if you need me and I would appreciate any information you can offer me. That's my girl in your hands. Take care of her for me," Jeremiah quietly asked. Tears cascaded now but Jeremiah continued to fight for composure.

Dr. Sousa turned to the two emergency room nurses working on Charlie Joe and said, "I'm going to go scrub in. I believe we will be in operating room number two. Theresa is the periop nurse working with me tonight. She's in house already. Please page her that I'm here and to go ahead and take Miss Bingham back. Anesthesia is waiting for us in the operating room." He then turned to Jeremiah and placed his hand on his back to guide him out of the emergency room. "I'll show you were you can wait while she is in surgery. It's on my way. Follow me."

38

Stuart Riedel sat with his youngest daughter, Rachelle, as the emergency room physician entered the small bay area. The physician closed the glass door and pulled the curtain so they could have some privacy. "My name is Dr. Hamid. I see that my nurse has already taken your blood pressure and pulse, Rachelle," she said as she sat on a rolling stool and faced them. Rachelle sat on her dad's lap in the chair next to the examination table. She looked at Stuart and asked, "Can you tell me how Rachelle is doing?"

"She's pretty quiet, doctor. I don't think she's hurt anywhere but given what she's gone through the last couple of hours, I'm worried she's in shock," Stuart offered.

"How are you feeling tonight, Rachelle?" Dr. Hamid asked as she took an ophthalmoscope from the wall and began to examine Rachelle's eyes.

Rachelle didn't answer Dr. Hamid. Instead, she pulled away from her and nestled closer to her daddy. Her doll and the decorative box clutched tight to her chest. Seeing her reaction, Dr. Hamid sat back on her rolling stool next to the chair where Stuart sat holding his daughter.

"It's not unusual for children to act this way after a traumatic event," Dr. Hamid began. "She doesn't appear to have any outward injuries and there are no obvious signs of shock at this time. The best thing for her right now is to give her time to process what she's experienced. Be supportive. Expect that her play might bring out some of her feelings about what she saw. It's important that you encourage her to talk about what happened, too, as it's all very therapeutic for her."

Stuart hugged Rachelle to his chest as he thought about all that she had gone through this night. He took a deep breath and let it out slowly before looking at Dr. Hamid. His wife was dead. He wasn't sure what

Rachelle had seen or heard, but he knew that life was going to be rough. Death left deep and invisible scars on survivors.

"I'm going to have my nurse give you contact information for a local psychiatrist who specializes in post-traumatic stress disorder and childhood trauma. I would suggest that you make an appointment to have Rachelle evaluated. I wouldn't expect you to have to take her more than a couple of times. It's really more to coach you on how best to help Rachelle deal with what happened," Dr. Hamid offered. "Is there anything else I can do for you before I leave?"

"We're good, doctor. Thank you," Stuart answered as he collected his daughter and stood to leave. His other daughter, Riley, had already been checked out and cleared to leave. His children were all safe, but he couldn't allow himself to start grieving for Shirley's death. He wanted to be alone for that, to let down and let go. Right now he needed to find a place for them to stay. Going home wasn't an option tonight.

***

Dr. Sousa had brought Jeremiah to the surgery waiting room and had promised to give him an update on Charlie Joe's condition as soon as he could. Jeremiah was impressed with Dr. Sousa's compassion. He had heard that surgeons usually had an awful bedside manner. The coffee pot with fresh coffee sat on a fully stocked refreshment cart in the corner of the room. Jeremiah helped himself to a cup as Stuart and his children wandered down the hall towards the hospital exit. Seeing Stuart, Jeremiah strode to the door and quietly called out, "Hey, Stuart!"

Hearing his name called, Stuart turned. He still held Rachelle in his arms. Kevin and Riley walked behind him.

Jeremiah came out of the room, coffee in hand. "Everyone doing okay?"

"The doctor checked everyone out. I'm taking the kids to a hotel for the rest of the night. Why are you still here? Are you waiting to see how Lance Meton comes through surgery?"

"Shaun, the guy you know as Spade, took my girlfriend hostage before coming after your family tonight. He beat her up pretty badly. She's in surgery now," Jeremiah replied. His hands shook as he spoke, and coffee spilled onto the floor. "I'm not sure why she became a target, other than she was at the wrong place at the wrong time."

"I'm sorry to hear that. Would you like us to stay with you until she gets out of surgery?" Stuart offered.

"We'd like to stay, Sheriff Stone. Lance is still in surgery, too. I heard in the emergency room that his mom was on her way over." Riley looked at her dad and asked, "Can we stay, dad? Please?"

Rachelle lifted her head off of Stuart's chest and looked at Jeremiah. She didn't say anything, but shifted her weight and lunged, arms outstretched towards him. Jeremiah caught her mid-fall.

"Hey, there now, little girl! What are you up to?" Jeremiah asked Rachelle.

Still holding her doll and decorative box, she put her little nose right up against his and answered. "Can we be friends?"

Stuart was shocked. It was the first thing Rachelle had said since yelling at the emergency room doctor.

Smiling, Jeremiah shifted Rachelle to his hip and said, "Of course we can be friends. What's in your box?"

"It's some letters my mommy wrote to my sister," Rachelle admitted. "I took them from the cabinet and hid them from the bad man."

Jeremiah looked at Stuart, not quite knowing what to say, or what to do.

Stuart's face had turned pale and he looked like he would pass out.

"Let's go in the waiting room and sit down for a few minutes. Kevin, why don't you help your Dad. He doesn't look very good,"

Jeremiah directed. He then led the way back into the empty surgery waiting room.

Jeremiah sat Rachelle down in the chair next to him. Rachelle popped off the chair and climbed up into his lap again.

"Will you read the letters to me? I can't read yet," Rachelle confessed as she handed the decorative box to him.

Her soft green eyes pleaded her case for her. Jeremiah thought, just for a moment, that Rachelle and Charlie Joe had the same colored eyes. Charlie Joe did the exact same thing when she wanted something from him. It was an odd thought. *Rachelle and Charlie Joe look a lot alike.*

Riley came over and sat next to Jeremiah. "How do you know the letters are for me, Rachelle?" she asked.

Stuart answered from across the room. "The letters aren't for you, Riley." He had his head in his hands as he spoke.

Riley had a quizzical look on her face as she turned to her brother, Kevin. Looking back at her dad, Riley wondered aloud. "Why would mom write letters to Rachelle?"

"Stuart," Jeremiah wasn't sure it was safe to ask this question in front of the kids, but he had to know. He waited for Stuart to turn and look at him before he continued. "Is there any chance that you and Shirley had another child? One that you gave up for adoption?"

Stuart turned and looked at Jeremiah. He couldn't speak, but the look on his face told the whole story. Both he and Jeremiah had put the pieces together at the same moment. Shaun had known that Charlie Joe was Stuart's daughter. Stuart had put Mombossa in jail, and once out, Shaun had been hired to take revenge. He had started with Charlie Joe. He came after the rest of the family, and because he loved the hunt, he had intentionally saved Charlie Joe for last.

Rachelle put her soft little hands on each side of Jeremiah's cheeks, turning his face towards hers. She said, "Mommy died. She's in heaven now with Jesus."

Rachelle was just a child: a child who just went through a very traumatic situation. Taking a deep breath, Jeremiah calmed himself. The family here in the room with him had been through a rough night. He kissed Rachelle on the forehead and gave her hug. "Yes. Your mommy died and is with Jesus, Rachelle. She's safe now."

"Mommy forgot to mail my letter to Santa, but Jesus took care of my sister anyway," Rachelle explained. "I put the letter in mommy's box so that my sister could see that I love her, too. I prayed the Jesus would keep her safe 'cause sometimes mommies and daddies can't take care of their babies. Right, Riley?"

Riley's eyes glistened with unshed tears as she remembered the story of the old man's wedding ring; the story that Rachelle liked to hear her tell. She reached over and stroked her sister's hair as she answered. "You're exactly right, Rachelle. Jesus took very good care of our sister. He's taking care of mommy now, too." A single tear escaped and slowly cascaded down her cheek as she offered Rachelle a weak smile.

39

One month later

Charlie Joe sat on her front porch swing wrapped in a wool blanket. The wind was calm, and the air crisp. Snow had fallen during the night and created a beautiful landscape of solitude all around her home. It was quiet, and peaceful. It was Charlie Joe's favorite time of year.

The surgery had gone without complications. Dr. Sousa was an excellent surgeon and had told her during her appointment the day before that she was healing beautifully. She would be able to start walking without crutches in two more weeks. The pain in her chest from her broken ribs was gone, and the fracture in her jaw was almost completely healed.

Jeremiah and Stuart Riedel had both been at her bedside when she came out of surgery. She was not shocked that Shaun had been the one behind the killings in Sweetwater. She was shocked to find out that Stuart and Shirley were her birth parents. There was no definitive proof, but the fact that Shaun had targeted her and Stuart's family was strong evidence. He was a man who made a living two ways: by acquiring information that no one else had access to, and killing people without leaving a trace of evidence. Given Shaun's history, she wasn't surprised at all.

Stuart had offered to do a blood test for DNA confirmation, but Charlie Joe had declined. Stuart had wanted to talk privately with her, but she had declined this as well. Instead, she took the box of letters that Rachelle, his youngest daughter, had hidden for her. The box sat in her lap, still unopened.

For the longest time Charlie Joe had wondered about her birth parents; why they gave her up, what they were like, if they had other children. The questions were endless. Now that the answers sat before her, she was afraid. Her whole life, she had had Jeremiah at her side. It was easy to be brave when someone loved you unconditionally; when that someone was there to cheer you on. Her excuse all these years to not marry him had been because she needed to know her past before she could face her future. Now that her past sat before her, she didn't know what to do with it.

Taking a deep breath, she opened the box, determined to read one letter. She would read one letter a day until she had read them all. She wanted to absorb what her birth mother left for her. She wanted to learn about her, how she thought, what she liked; but most of all she wanted to know why she gave her up for adoption.

The first letter was folded tightly and had scribbles all over it written with crayon. There were some drawings of a spade in black crayon. *This must be Rachelle's letter to Santa that her mom forgot to mail,* she thought. Jeremiah had told her the story about Rachelle asking Santa to pray for her. A monster with spades on his arms was going to try to hurt her, and Jesus and told Rachelle to pray for her sister. It was a sweet gesture, asking Santa to pray for her, and one she would forever treasure. The fact that there were scribbles instead of words made the letter that much more precious.

Charlie Joe refolded the letter and set it aside. The next letter was dated December, only a few weeks ago. It was the last letter her birth mother wrote before she died. She wanted to start at the beginning, with the first letter so she refolded it and put it back. Reaching for the bottom of the pile, Charlie Joe found the letter she was looking for. It, too, was dated December, but the year was the year of her birth. *Shirley had pretty handwriting*, she thought as she began reading.

Dear Charlie Joe,

My name is Shirley Alexander. I am 20 years old and getting ready to graduate from college next year. Your daddy, Stuart Riedel and I met in college at a party two years ago. We fell in love but wanted to wait until we graduated before we got married. We both are still in college and can barely afford to feed ourselves and pay rent. We want a better life for you than the one that we can offer. It hurts me to give you up for adoption. I love you so much. Sometimes doing the right thing for someone else is more painful than doing what would be easier for me. I can't think about what I want, though. I have to think about you, the life your adoptive parents can give you and the opportunities you will have if I do this.

I have worked with a judge who was friends with my daddy. He found a wonderful couple that is childless. They are kind, and loving. Your new mommy fell in love with you the moment she held you. It broke my heart to let you go, but my soul sings knowing that you will be clothed in daily love. They are good people and have promised to keep your given name of Charlie Joe. I named you after my granddaddy. He loved nature and was quite the rascal. If you are anything like him, you will be full of character and kindness.

I promise to pray for you every day. I promise to write you a letter every year. I promise to love you forever.

Love,

Shirley

Charlie Joe had trouble seeing the last lines of the letter. Tears had clouded her vision. She hadn't heard Jeremiah drive up her snow-covered driveway. He was standing at the foot of her porch stairs watching her when she noticed him.

"How long have you been standing there snooping on me, Mr. Stone?" she demanded as she wiped a tear from her cheek.

"Long enough, Miss Bingham," he countered with a smile. His hand was on the banister, but he waited to be invited onto the porch. It was a cold morning. His breath froze in the air.

"Well are you going to stand there and stare at me all day or are you going to come up here and help me back into the house? I'm frozen solid," she complained. "One of my crutches fell off the porch and I can't reach it."

Jeremiah Stone's smile spread across his entire face as he leapt up the stairs and strode towards where she was sitting on the porch swing. "It's a beautiful morning, isn't it?" he offered as he sat down beside her. He ignored the fact that one of her crutches was out of reach. She didn't need them when he was around.

"It is a beautiful morning. One that should be enjoyed by an open fire and not frozen on a porch swing," she stated. "You said you'd be here an hour ago. You're late."

Jeremiah knew Charlie Joe. She didn't want him to see her cry so she pretended to be mad to cover up her tears. It was a ploy she had used on him many times before and it wasn't going to work today. "I said I'd be here at exactly ten o'clock. I'm never late."

"I'm not talking to you until we go inside. It's insane to sit out here when it's this cold," she stated.

Jeremiah gave a little chuckle, stood up and then got down on one knee in front of her. "I just have one question to ask you, Charlie Joe. You can wait."

"Jeremiah Stone, you take me inside this minute," she demanded.

"Charlie Joe, I'm not going to carry you inside until you answer my question."

"Well ask it then!"

Jeremiah pulled his great grandmother's ring out of his pocket and offered it to her. "Charlie Joe, you drive me absolutely insane when I'm around you. I love you. I want to spend the rest of my life with you," he said.

Charlie Joe knew this was coming. He drove her as crazy as she drove him, and they both loved their lives together. "I'm making waffles for breakfast. Do you want bacon? I love bacon."

"Charlie Joe, I'm serious. I want to know if you are going to marry me or not. Answer me!"

Smiling, she looked at him. He had that same boyish look he had when they were stealing watermelons after church on Sundays. She loved him more than anything in the world, and couldn't imagine her life without him. Maybe that's what her birth mother felt for her husband, Stuart. Wanting the best for someone you loved wasn't a crime. It was a gift, a beautiful gift. She wanted to get to know her birth family. She wanted a family of her own. Being Jeremiah's wife was something she had wanted for a long time.

"I would be proud to be your wife, Jeremiah," she answered. "Can we get married in the spring? I love flowers and the hills are so pretty in the spring."

Jeremiah scooped her up off of the porch swing and swung her around.

"Miss Bingham, I'll give you whatever you want," he admitted before kissing her and taking her inside.

The End

Don't miss out!

Visit the website below and you can sign up to receive emails whenever Heather Rhodes publishes a new book. There's no charge and no obligation.

https://books2read.com/r/B-A-LFQAB-VBMOC

BOOKS 2 READ

Connecting independent readers to independent writers.

Also by Heather Rhodes

Forging Friendships
Sweetwater Secrets

Watch for more at https://calmjourney.org/.

About the Author

Heather Rhodes is a writer, educator, and nurse practitioner. She loves connecting with people and helping them achieve their life goals one step at a time. She is passionate about living a sacred life, connected to God, others, and nature. She considers gratefulness and acts of service a necessity for a happy life.

Read more at https://calmjourney.org/.

www.ingramcontent.com/pod-product-compliance
Lightning Source LLC
Chambersburg PA
CBHW032144020726
47496CB00003B/713